After School Club

Starring Alex . . .

. . . as the girl with the voice of an angel
(who can be a little devil too)

Helena Pielichaty
Illustrated by Melanie Williamson

OXFORD
UNIVERSITY PRESS

OXFORD
UNIVERSITY PRESS

Great Clarendon Street, Oxford OX2 6DP

Oxford University Press is a department of the University of Oxford.
It furthers the University's objective of excellence in research, scholarship,
and education by publishing worldwide in

Oxford New York

Auckland Bangkok Buenos Aires Cape Town
Chennai Dar es Salaam Delhi Hong Kong Istanbul Karachi
Kolkata Kuala Lumpur Madrid Melbourne Mexico City Mumbai
Nairobi São Paulo Shanghai Taipei Tokyo Toronto

Oxford is a registered trade mark of Oxford University Press
in the UK and in certain other countries

British Library Cataloguing in Publication Data available

ISBN 0-19-275249-9

1 3 5 7 9 10 8 6 4 2

Designed and typeset by Mike Brain Graphic Design Limited, Oxford

Printed in Great Britain by Cox & Wyman Ltd, Reading, Berkshire

to my niece Claudia Agnieska Pielichaty
with love

with many thanks to Elaine (again!)

Welcome to

ZAPS

Contact: Jan Fryston NNEB (Supervisor)
on 07734-090876 for details.

Please note: Mr Sharkey, headmaster of Zetland Avenue
Primary School, politely requests parents/carers <u>not</u> to
contact the school directly as the After School Club is
independent of the school and he wants it to stay that way!

All children must be registered before they attend.

Zetland Avenue Primary School (ZAPS) After School Club

Newsletter

Dear Parents and Carers,

We have lots of exciting things planned for this year and hope you will tell your friends and neighbours all about us. Children do not have to attend Zetland Avenue Primary School to come to After School Club; any child is welcome as long as they are aged between five and eleven and have been registered.

Special Events:

1. November: **Children in Need Fundraising.** We will be joining in with the main school's activities. We wonder what Mr Sharkey will be getting up to this year? (If you remember, last year he sat in a bath of smelly jelly!)

2. February half-term holiday: **Film-making Week.** Media Studies students from Bretton Hill College will be showing us how to make and star in a real film. Watch out, Hollywood!

3. Easter: **Pop Kids.** We will be staging a talent show to perform in front of parents and carers.

4. Summer: **Get Active!** Summer Sports activities for everyone throughout the holidays.

Also:

E-PALS

Once the new computers have been installed we are hoping to set up an Internet connection to After School Clubs throughout the UK. Children who are interested will be able to write to their 'E-pals' from Penzance to Pitlochry!

See you all soon,

Jan

Jan Fryston (Supervisor)

After School Club

Sammie Wesley

Reggie Glazzard

Alex McCormack

Lloyd Fountain

Mrs Fryston
Supervisor

Mrs McCormack
Assistant

Brody Miller

Sam Riley

Jolene Nevin

Brandon Petty

Some comments from our customers at the After School Club:

'It's better than going round my gran's and having to watch Kung Fu films all day in the holidays'—

Brandon Petty, Y1

'It's good because I am home-schooled so the After School Club gives me a chance to mix with children my own age and make new friends.'

Lloyd Fountain, aged 9

'I love going to ZAPS After School Club— there's so much to do. It's a blast.'

(Brody Miller, Y6)

— You feel at ease
— On the purple settees
— The staff are kind
— And help you unwind
— So come along
— You can't go wrong

— (Sam Riley, Y5)

'After School Club is OK, apart from the rats and poisonous biscuits.' (Don't worry folks – just messing with your minds – Ha! Ha!)

Reggie G. aged 133*

*our resident comedian informs me he prefers to use months to describe his age – JF

'There's not nowhere better than After School Club and I like Mrs Fryston because she is kind and understands how you feel about things.'

Sammie Wesley Y5

'I've been to other After School Clubs before but they've been rubbish and I've always been kicked out but this one is the best.'

Jolene Nevin Y5

'I have been coming to After School Club since it started because my mum is one of the helpers. I enjoy the craft activities and when new people start, like Jolene.'

Alex McCormack Y4

What do you think? Add your own comment

Chapter One

My name is Alexandra Mary McCormack—Alex for short. If I had been a boy, I would have been called Daniel Timothy McCormack, after my brother who died before I was born, so I'm glad I'm a girl. It's bad enough being surrounded by him without being named after him too. Dead Daniel is everywhere in our house. I'm not trying to be disrespectful or anything but for someone who's not been around for ten years, and was only four when he died, that boy takes up way too much space. There are pictures of him on nearly every wall, with his halo of curly hair and huge blue eyes staring out at you as if to say 'Who are you?' Where there isn't a photograph, there's one of his drawings from nursery school.

What used to be his bedroom, and everyone except Mum now calls the den, is *still* full of his toys and even the garden has a bench dedicated to him. Worst of all, every night before I go to bed, I have to say goodnight to his ashes that are on the mantelpiece. I'm not kidding—talk about creepy. The only good thing about the ashes business is watching visitors' faces fall when they ask what is in the nice lacquered box and Mum says 'My son'.

Which brings me on to the other gripe I have. Visitors. Number Twelve Zetland Avenue is a magnet for them. Dad says that if he had a pound for every time the kettle boiled he'd be the richest man in Europe. Mum just tuts and tells him to stop exaggerating but it's true. There's always some sort of support group or other downstairs—Bereaved Parents, St Rose's Children's Hospice, the Meningitis Awareness Group. Tonight it's the After School Club Committee which isn't a support group, exactly, but it's the same difference.

After School club—as if I don't see enough of the place. I know I'm sounding a grade A whinger but how would you like it if on top of doing a full day at school and three hours at After School club and only having a rubbish fry-up before everyone arrived at seven, you were sent upstairs to 'entertain' yourself instead of being able to watch your favourite TV programme? It wouldn't be so bad if I had my own telly but I don't so I have spent most of the evening in my bedroom doing my Easter Garden for Sunday School. Even that's a disaster and I'm usually good at creative things. I'm very unhappy with my crosses. I've used lollipop sticks but they won't stay upright and keep toppling over as if they've been in a hurricane. I won't be able to put it on display next week at this rate.

My sister, Caitlin, is in the bedroom next to mine and I'd like to ask her for help but I'm not supposed to disturb her. Caitlin is sixteen and a sixth former at The Magna and is under a lot of pressure with exams. I can't wait to be sixteen and under a lot of pressure. You get out of doing chores because you've always got essays and you don't have to go shopping on Saturdays because you have a Saturday job and you don't have to go to church on Sundays because you stop believing in God and sleep until lunchtime instead. It's such a cushy life.

Caitlin must have finished her homework because I

could now hear Beethoven wailing through the wall. Seconds later there was a quick tap on my door and she stuck her head round and grinned at me. 'Go make us a cup of tea, Alex,' she said.

'N-o spells no.'

'Go on,' she repeated, opening the door wider and leaning her head to one side as if that was going to persuade me, especially with that hairstyle. Like me she has straight, light-brown hair, but as usual hers was scraped back in a tight, ugly ponytail that did nothing for her.

'Why do I have to do it? You're the one that's thirsty,' I pointed out.

'Because I have a psychology essay to finish then I've got to practise for band tomorrow, kind, sweet little sister of mine,' she whined.

I felt insulted. 'I am not kind and sweet,' I complained.

But she was already disappearing back to her room. 'And nab me a few biscuits—shortbread preferably,' she called over her shoulder.

I sighed and headed downstairs. I didn't really mind making her a cup of tea. I liked doing grown-up things like that. She had no chance on the biscuit

4

front, though. I knew for a fact the shortbread wouldn't have lasted two seconds—Jan This liked them the most.

'Jan This' was my secret name for Mrs Fryston, the After School club supervisor. She's Mum's boss. Mum *loves* her. 'Jan said this' and 'Jan does that' is all we ever hear. I don't know why she's so impressed by Mrs Fryston. All Mrs Fryston does is fill in forms and suck up to the parents. It's my mum that does all the hard work at ZAPS After School club in my opinion. I bet she was volunteering this second to mend something or buy something or paint something for that shabby mobile hut, as if she's nothing else to do.

To prove it, I stopped by the half-open door of the living room as I passed on my way to the kitchen, hiding behind the bulging coats draped over the hat stand. I peered through the gap and could just make out a bunch of heads above the backs of the chairs. Mrs Fryston was talking and Tanis Fountain, Lloyd's mum, was nodding in agreement. Of all the parents there, I knew Tanis best because she's my Sunday School teacher. I don't mind her at all because she is always cheerful, which makes a change from most of our visitors.

'So, to re-cap,' Mrs Fryston banged on, 'I'll

continue setting up the e-pals project with links to other clubs. Sarah, you'll organize the sound equipment for the Pop Kids event next week and Ann, you're going to update all the registration details for us by Friday. Are you sure you don't want someone to give you a hand?'

Mum—she's Ann—looked up and shook her head. 'I'll be fine,' she said. Told you she'd get roped into something. Update all the registration details. Blinking Norah—Mrs Fryston didn't mean onto computer, did she? That would take Mum years. I peered closer. She was doing the notes again. Minutes, they're called, but they don't take her minutes to type up—she is the world's slowest typist, though she pretends she's not.

Mrs Fryston smiled at everyone, adjusted her silky neck-scarf against her fitted grey jacket as she turned from one member to the other. She does have good dress sense, I'll give her that. It's a pity it doesn't rub off a bit on Mum, who was in her horrible belted dress and bobbly cream cardy Grandma had knitted her for Christmas. It had one arm longer than the other so she had to keep the sleeves rolled up hoping no one could tell. No make-up, no jewellery. That's my mum.

'Well,' the Boss continued, 'that just leaves me to

6

thank Ann for letting us use her house again and to thank you all for coming. Dates to suit for the next meeting?' There was a flurry as they all dived for their diaries. No prizes for guessing where the meeting would be. I headed towards the kitchen and hoped they'd all leave quickly.

The kitchen was a right tip. All the dinner pots were still piled up because Mum hadn't had time to sort them before the meeting. Something black and disgusting floated in the grill pan that had been left to soak on the worktop. Nearby, the flip-top bin, unable to flip because it was stuffed full of rubbish, gave off a nasty fishy smell that had been getting nastier and fishier all week. I ignored it all and went to fill the water filter jug from the tap. I could hear  people leaving and shouting 'Bye' and 'See you' and finally the front door closing. I let out a huge sigh of relief as I heard footsteps approach.

'I'm glad that's over. I suppose that lazy old meanie has lumbered you with all the work again,' I called over my shoulder to Mum.

'Hello, Alex,' the lazy old meanie replied instead.

Chapter Two

Oops! I swung round with the jug in my hand, tipping water over the rim so it wet my top. 'Hello, Mrs Fryston,' I greeted her, fixing a big smile on my face and trying to pretend I had not said what I had just said.

'Where shall I put this?' she asked, indicating the tray full of beakers and plates she was carrying. The biscuit plate was empty, as I predicted.

'Erm . . . over there,' I said, pointing to the breakfast bar which just had enough space to take the tray if she budged up the wash basket full of damp clothes waiting their turn in the tumble drier.

She smiled at me again and

nodded towards the teapot I was emptying. 'Is there anything I can do to help? My lift's not here yet.'

'Not really,' I replied, now pouring water into the kettle.

She launched straight into her mind-reading act. 'I'm sorry if you've had to hide away during our meeting. It's just so much nicer sitting on comfortable chairs than squatting down on kiddies' ones for an hour and with you living just over the road from the school, it's so convenient . . .'

If she thought I was going to say, 'It doesn't matter', she had another think coming. 'I suppose so,' I said instead.

Mrs Fryston looked intently at me. '"So convenient." That sounded awful, didn't it? But your mum *does* insist.'

'I know,' I sighed.

She changed the subject. 'What do you think of the e-pals idea?'

I looked at her blankly, in case she had seen me eavesdropping and was trying to catch me out. 'That we started this afternoon? Making links with children from other After School clubs throughout the country? You filled in your "About Me" details, didn't you?' she prompted.

'Oh, yes,' I said hastily, 'I sent mine to the website's notice-board thing.'

'That's good. You might get a reply tomorrow,' she said, reaching out for an already dry cereal bowl and wiping it with a flourish.

I doubted I would get a reply. I had made my details as boring as possible so that nobody would want to write to me. It wasn't my kind of thing, e-mailing.

She must have been able to tell I wasn't that keen because she changed the subject again. 'What about the Pop Kids theme during the holidays? Are you looking forward to that?'

'Not really,' I admitted.

'No? I thought it would be right up your street. I have heard you're quite a singer,' she stated. 'Mr Sharkey was telling me how you're the star of his choir.'

'Not really,' I repeated and began to measure tea leaves into the pot. Two and a half spoonfuls. Two's not enough and three's too much. Jan This nudged me lightly in the side, trying to show how friendly she was but only annoying me instead. 'Now don't be modest, Alex.'

I shrugged. 'I'm not being! It's just that everyone

else is so rubbish so it makes me sound better than I am. Anyway, I don't know any pop songs. I only know traditional folk songs and hymns.'

'Oh,' she said shortly.

Luckily Mum came in to rescue me from any further divvy conversation and told Jan This that Andrew had arrived. 'On time, as usual,' she said, giving her this knowing look. Andrew was Mr Sharkey, my headteacher, and they're going out. I knew ages before anyone. I suppose if there is one advantage to having a mum who works at the After School club it is that you get all the inside information. They've been going out for about four months now but it's only just become common knowledge. It's not going smoothly, either, I can tell you, because of his mean ex-wife and her mardy teenage daughters, Kate and Anna.

I opened the fridge door quietly and took ages pretending to look for the milk. These were the times I found out more than I should, and pretending to be concentrating on something else helped no end, but this time Mrs Fryston just said goodbye and that was that.

I asked Mum if she wanted a cup of tea.

'Erm, no thanks,' Mum said, frowning and looking

worriedly at her notebook, 'I want to get going on these records. Jan needs them as soon as possible.'

'Do you have to? I wanted to watch telly with you.' I hated watching telly on my own. It made me feel lonely.

'What?' she said, looking at me but not looking at me, if you know what I mean. I repeated what I'd said but she shook her head. 'No, not tonight, Alex. I've got to get on,' she replied, then bit her lip. 'Must you wear that when we've got visitors?' she asked.

We both glanced down at my short, tight top with 'Bad Girl' printed across the chest. It was one of a set

 I had bought with my Christmas vouchers in the January sales— asking for vouchers is the only way to make sure I get decent things. Each of my tops had a different slogan like 'Bad Girl', 'Talk to the Hand', 'Whatever', and 'Up for It'—nothing rude or half as suggestive as I could have got but my old-fashioned mum disliked every one of them. 'What's wrong with it now?' I demanded.

Mum's frown deepened so that her forehead

crumpled with even more worry lines than usual. 'You'll catch such a cold,' she fussed. 'I'm sure things like that are meant to be worn under a jumper, like a vest.'

'How would you know?' I retorted, getting annoyed that the only conversation we had had all evening was where she has a go at me. 'You don't know anything about what girls wear nowadays, so don't think you can start now!'

I would never have been so cheeky to Mum if Caitlin or Dad had been around but I knew I could get away with it on a one-to-one. Mum never tells me off—she's such a pushover. 'You're right,' she agreed readily, 'I don't, but . . .'

I'd had enough. I gave her a dirty look and took Caitlin's tea and stormed out of the kitchen. I dumped Caitlin's drink next to where she was working at her desk, told her there weren't any biscuits left, and walked out. She said thanks and that I was 'a gem' but she had gone into 'essay world' and barely noticed me really.

I sat alone in my room for ages feeling sorry for myself but then I got bored so I went back to my Easter Garden. I decided to ignore the wobbly crosses and focus on the green hill instead. Mr Pisarski who ran the grocery shop six doors down had given me a piece of that imitation grass stuff he used to display his vegetables. It looked really effective yesterday when I had stuck it down over a plant pot but now I wasn't so sure. I reckoned the grass looked a bit long, so I took out my nail scissors and began clipping away. I must have been really engrossed because I didn't even know Dad was behind me until I felt a pair of cold hands tickle the back of my neck, making me nearly jump out of my skin.

I told him off for nearly scaring me to death, then gave him a hug, folding my arms round his big tummy and not letting go for ages. 'And how's my little nightingale today?' he asked, hugging me back.

I looked up at him, with his handsome, smooth face and grey-flecked hair that would be a mass of frizzy curls like Daniel's if he didn't keep it cut so short, and felt happy he was home. I liked my dad; he was always calm. 'Not bad under the circumstances,' I informed him.

He wiggled his thick, dark eyebrows. 'Well, that's good enough for me. Are you coming down for some supper? There are rumours of cheese on toast,' he said, loosening his stripy tie.

Cheese on toast? That was a good sign. Someone must have washed the grill pan. I dropped the scissors and followed him out.

Chapter Three

Downstairs, all the McCormacks were together at last. Caitlin was watching TV in one armchair and Mum was checking through her notebook in the other and I sat on the sofa and shared Dad's cheese toastie. He talked about a Georgian house he'd valued on St John's Square and how fantastic it was—Dad's an estate agent and knows all there is to know about property—and I listened. If I didn't make it as a fashion expert when I was older, I had being an estate agent down as a back-up. 'Did it have all its original features?' I asked.

'It did—right down to servants' bells in the cellars.'

'Oh—servants' bells!' I gasped, my imagination running wild. 'I'd love those.'

'Don't give her ideas,' Caitlin muttered from her chair.

'Excuse me, this is a business conversation, lassie,' I told her, and asked Dad what price he'd valued the property at. I whistled when he told me. 'Could we afford that?'

'In your dreams,' Caitlin said, flicking through the TV guide. Funny way to do a psychology essay, if you ask me.

Dad agreed with her. 'Not in a million years,' he sighed, biting deep into his toastie so the cheese oozed like Red Leicester lava.

'Well, even if we could afford it, we'd never leave here,' Mum added.

I looked at her curiously, surprised she had even been listening. 'Why not?' I asked because I'd love to live somewhere else. Somewhere detached and away from a main road so the windows didn't rattle every time a lorry went past and somewhere so remote nobody could be faffed to drive out there for a meeting. Somewhere very *inconvenient*.

Mum glanced across at me and gave me a weak, far-off smile. 'Oh, I could never leave here. All my memories are here,' she said, her eyes flicking over to the fireplace.

'But if we moved, you could have new memories,' I pointed out and would have said more, but Dad

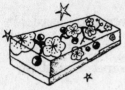 nudged me and pursed his mouth in such a way I knew I had to belt up.

'So, what's on telly, Cate old mate?' he asked abruptly, changing the subject oh-so-obviously. 'Anything interesting?'

'Well, given that we have a choice of over two hundred channels . . .' Caitlin replied, pressing the remote so the menu flashed on the screen, 'not a lot.'

'No,' Mum continued, 'I'd never leave here. Never.' There was a catch in her voice, as if she was on the verge of tears.

Caitlin looked guardedly at Dad then began to flick furiously from one channel to another.

'Oh, switch the thing off!' Dad ordered jovially. 'Alex will entertain us, won't you? Give us a song, pal.'

'I don't feel like it.'

'Go on—for your old man after a hard day at work. Banish my tense, nervous headache.'

He suddenly flopped sideways across me, rubbing a mock headache with his hand and looking silly.

'The only way I'm ever leaving here is in a wooden box,' Mum informed no one in particular, 'that's the only way.'

When she started talking like that, all morose and

maudlin, we all knew it was time for distraction tactics. I shoved Dad off me and stood up, found my place bang in the middle row of the zigzags on the hearthrug, and took a deep breath. I began with Dad's favourite, 'Speed Bonny Boat', singing softly but clearly like Mr Sharkey had taught us. My voice echoed round the room and the more I sang, the more everyone relaxed. Dad leaned contentedly against the cushions and closed his eyes, Caitlin hummed along and Mum watched. She watched and listened and little by little her face lost its anxious appearance so that she looked younger and almost pretty.

After three songs, my throat began to tickle, so I gave up and collapsed onto the sofa. Everyone gave me a round of applause and I jumped up again and took a bow. 'The voice of an angel!' Dad cried. 'Despite evidence to the contrary!'

After that we watched a repeat of *Only Fools and Horses* and then it was my bedtime. ''Night,' I said, addressing everyone in turn.

'Goodnight, Alex,' Mum said, before coming out with the words I dreaded. 'Don't forget to kiss Daniel.'

I swallowed hard, knowing there was no way out of this one. We all kissed Daniel goodnight, no matter what.

I approached the mantelpiece solemnly, careful not to let my shins touch the bar of the electric fire, even though it was  only on low. I breathed in deeply and stared at the bluey-turquoise lacquered box in the centre of the marble shelf where Dead Daniel rested.

Everything surrounding the box—the school photo of me on one side, the school photo of Caitlin on the other, the two wooden elephants, and even Mum's bottles of tablets—had a light coating of dust over them—but not the box. It gleamed so much from where Mum polished it every day, the glare from the light-fitting in the ceiling bounced off it, making me blink.

I so hated this. 'Goodnight, Daniel,' I whispered, my heart thudding against my ribs, my stomach heaving as I leaned forward and kissed him as quickly as I could and dashed upstairs to bed.

Chapter Four

Next day started off the usual way. Breakfast round the table with Dad in his suit and Caitlin in a book and Mum still in her dressing gown. Mornings are not Mum's best time of day. She has these tablets to help her sleep and they can take a while to wear off.

Dad leaves first, then Caitlin, then me. Since I have been in Year Four, I have been allowed to go to school on my own because it is only over the road and there is a crossing lady called Mrs Beamish to show me across.

In class—I'm in Miss Coupland's—I sat right at the back with my best friend, Jennifer Wilkinson. We are allowed to sit at the back because we don't mess about or anything. I like to just get on with my work and Jenny does too, so we make good partners. I'm as good as gold in school. It's *after* school I have trouble with.

At half-past three Mum arrived to escort me and the other After School club attendees across the playground. She was holding Brandon Petty by one hand and another kid from Reception by the other. That annoyed me straight off so I ran ahead of the group to get to the mobile first, ignoring her when she told me to wait because she hadn't called for Mr Idle's class yet.

It was Tuesday, which is a fairly quiet day at the club, so I didn't mind going as much. The mobile is not big enough sometimes, especially if it is wet out and there isn't an outside activity going on. I hate it then. The windows get all steamed up and the air feels heavy and thick, like an old man's coat. On Tuesdays, though, there are usually only about nine or ten regulars, so everyone has first choice of activities, no matter what the weather. Not that it makes much difference to me—I always choose the activity Mum's running. Partly it is because she does all the art and craft side and that's my favourite anyway but partly it is to keep an eye on her. She tends to fuss too much round the little ones and she gets carried away with them if you don't watch her.

Today I planned to get started straightaway on the necklace I had begun. I was halfway through a choker-design using tiny orange and lemon beads which were dead fiddly to thread onto cotton. I really wanted to have it finished so I could wear it to Sunday School but Jan This didn't even give me time to dump my sandwich box in the cloakroom before she called me across to the computers. Now what? I thought as I trundled my way towards her.

The usual gang were already huddled over three of the computers—Lloyd Fountain, Brody Miller, and Reggie Glazzard. Reggie Glazzard's dad had recently donated two brand new computers from his firm, to help Mrs Fryston set up this e-pal project. I reckon it was more of a guilt thing—someone must have tipped Mr Glazzard off about how his son hogged the computer area all the time and he felt bad about it.

'You've got an e-mail!' Mrs Fryston beamed at me and pointed to the vacant screen which had a picture of an unopened envelope in one corner with 'Mail for Alex' written by the side. 'You're the first one!'

'Does she get a prize?' Reggie asked, pushing his glasses up the bridge of his nose.

Then Brody, his girlfriend, said to me, 'I hate you! I spent ages and ages on my details but I haven't had

23

one lousy response,' and smiled at me in a way that showed she wasn't at all bothered.

You do know who I mean when I talk about Brody Miller, don't you? If you don't, just go out of your house and find the nearest bus shelter and look at the poster plastered all over the side hoarding. The girl modelling on it—with the beautiful long red hair and wearing the latest swanky range of Funky Punk clothes—that's Brody Miller.

'Who's written to me?' I asked in disbelief remembering what rubbish I had put.

'Open it and find out,' Mrs Fryston instructed.

I leaned forward, scowling, and clicked on the envelope. *'Dear Alex,'* it began, *'My name is Courtney Long and I go to Burnside Primary After School club in Washington Tyne and Wear. I am not writing this because I want to be your e-pal because I already have 1 in Preston and 1 in Isleworth. Someone else here wants to*  *write to you but she's making me write to you first. She sez she knows you but isn't sure if you want to get in touch. Her name is Jolene Nevin and her e-mail is footygirl@burnsideasc/educ/co.uk. Write to her soon pleeeeease and stop her doing my head in? CL.'*

'Huh!' I snorted and turned round to find everyone staring at me over my shoulder.

'Oh, cool!' Brody said, not even pretending she hadn't read my letter. 'Are you going to write back?'

'Not in a million years,' I said immediately and left them all staring.

Chapter Five

'You'll never guess who I've just had an e-mail from?' I said to Mum as I sat down at the craft table and pulled the bead tray across to me.

'Who?' she said, cutting round a picture of a skateboard and handing it to Brandon, her only customer, to stick on his sugar paper.

'That Jolene! Well, sort of.'

'Really?' Mum frowned.

'Jolene the bad girl?' Brandon asked.

I shot him a warning look to keep his crusty nose out but he was too busy picking glue off his fingers to notice.

'What did she say?' Mum asked.

'Nothing yet—she was just asking if she could write to me.'

Brandon stuck his oar in again. 'She was nasty. She broke Brody's tooth and made her cry.'

It was true. It's a long story but basically, Jolene, who is Brody's niece, had got into an argument with Brody last half-term holiday and pushed her down the steps outside. I was there and saw it all. She pushed her so hard Brody went flying and smashed her tooth; that's a double-disaster because she's a model, remember. There was blood everywhere and for days afterwards I could see Brody fall and hear the sound she made when she hit the ground. Horrible.

The sad thing was, up until then I had really, really liked Jolene, even though she had only been coming to the club a few days. We just got on mega well right from the start and were becoming really close but when Jolene lost her temper like that, I knew it was over. I hate loud rows and scenes of any sort—they scare me. There's no way I could be friendly with someone like that. She wrote me a letter afterwards but that went straight in the bin.

'Well, it's up to you,' Mum said, 'though I never liked the girl. She was a bad influence on you.'

'Exactly,' I said, agreeing with her for once.

Brandon grabbed a handful of lentils and tried to scatter them across his picture but most of them stuck to his fingers, making him look as if he had orange fungus growing out of them. 'There—I've finished!' he announced.

'It's wonderful,' Mum smiled. I wished she wouldn't lie to him. It only encourages him to come back. The thing she just couldn't see about Brandon Petty was that he was really, really irritating. After the Brody–Jolene incident, when I'd been shaken up, I tried to be nice to everyone, including Brandon. I even bought him his favourite green sweets a couple of times but the novelty wore off after about a week. I just couldn't keep up the pretence of liking the little squirt.

Now he was creeping round Mum. 'You can have it, Mrs 'Cormick,' he announced, holding the soggy sheet out towards her.

Her face went pink for some stupid reason. 'Oh, Brandon, are you sure? Maybe your mummy would like it?' she said, her eyes shining.

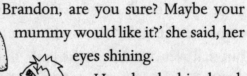

He shook his head. 'Nah! Mummy says she's got enough rubbish. She throws them straight in the bin.'

'Well, I'll definitely keep it then,' Mum said gently, carrying the picture to the drying rack so carefully you would have thought it was a tray of priceless diamonds.

'Go do something else now,' I told Brandon sharply.

'Like what?' he asked, scowling back at me through his long, tangled fringe.

'Like getting lost,' I hissed.

'You're a nasty-pasty,' he said and stuck his tongue out at me.

'Back at you,' I snarled.

That got rid of him. He slid from the chair and ambled over to pester Sam and Sammie at the tuck shop instead.

Soon it was the end of the session and I had to help Mum clear away, then wait until everyone was collected. Brody's mum, Kiersten, arrived first, breezing in and smiling broadly at everyone. She used to be a model too and is still really, really beautiful. I always take note of what she is wearing so I can copy her style when in I'm in my thirties and old. Today she had on smart black trousers with a plain white shirt and pointy shoes. Simple but classic.

Sammie Wesley's mum was last to arrive, as usual. Mrs Wesley is really overweight and dyes her hair too much but even she wears trendy clothes. My mum, as usual, looked really boring and drab next to all of them. I sometimes felt as if I had been born to the wrong family.

Chapter Six

The house was empty by the time Mum and I returned from After School club but I knew Caitlin had been in earlier from the whiff of burnt toast in the air. Mum went to put the kettle on and I read a note Caitlin had left by the phone to say she was at band practice and would be back about nine and Dad would be picking her up. Beneath it was a list of missed calls for Mum. 'Caitlin's at band—Dad's picking her up,' I relayed.

'What soup do you want? Tomato or chicken noodle?' Mum asked, standing on tiptoes to reach up into the cupboard, her underskirt at half-mast.

'I don't mind,' I said.

A packet of chicken noodle came flying down. 'Here you go, love. Can you make it yourself? The sooner I finish those records the better—I only managed four last night. There's plenty of cheese and ham in the fridge for sandwiches.'

'OK,' I said dully. I would have liked a bit of attention, especially as she was supposed to have a free night tonight. Instead, she headed for the door with her hastily made mug of coffee, before pausing by the worktop. I thought she had changed her mind and was going to have something to eat with me at least, but no.

'Isn't this sweet?' she said, pointing to Brandon Petty's gunk she had brought home with us. 'Fancy his mother throwing his things in the bin. I always kept everything of Daniel's.'

'Did you keep everything of mine?' I asked immediately.

She looked at me blankly. 'What? Oh, I'm sure I did. I can't really remember.'

'Where are they?'

'What?'

'All my paintings from when I was five?'

Mum glanced back to the lentil-laden sugar paper and seemed flustered. 'I don't know—ask your father when he comes home,' she said, creasing her thick eyebrows together so that they puckered unflatteringly. 'They'll be somewhere—in the loft maybe?' She glanced from me to the wall clock, told me to be careful when I heated the soup on the hob, then went upstairs.

That left me feeling really hurt and angry. It didn't matter that I knew exactly where my drawings and paintings were from when I was five. They were where they had always been—in the bottom drawer beneath my cabin bed. What mattered was that she so obviously didn't have a clue. I stared hard at Brandon's picture for a second, then rolled it up roughly and took it out to the dustbin where I squashed it into an empty box of washing powder and then covered it with bean cans. 'Stick lentils on that, creep,' I muttered triumphantly.

I was just washing my hands and feeling a lot better when the phone rang. It was some bloke from the meningitis group. That's what Daniel died from. I don't know much about meningitis except one of the symptoms is if you've got a rash, the rash doesn't go away if you roll a glass over it. Something like that. 'I've called twice already,' the man said accusingly.

'We've only just got in one second ago,' I retorted.

Honestly—some people.

Even Mum looked perturbed when I went upstairs to give her the message. 'Oh, dear. If it's Jeff I'll be on forever. I'll never get this done by Friday.' She prodded a key with her left index finger, then prodded another with her right. 'Will you save this for me, Alex?'

'I suppose so. I have to do everything else around here,' I replied as she hurried downstairs.

I quickly pressed the disc icon on the toolbar to save the work. I could see she had hardly transferred anything on to it from the hand-written sheet nearby. On the screen, the grids under the heading 'Samantha Wesley Registration Details' were mostly empty apart from her address and date of birth.

I picked up the sheet and began to read. I knew I shouldn't really—registration forms were confidential but I had never looked at one close-up before. It was funny seeing Sammie's full name written out as Samantha Louise. At least it wasn't an embarrassing middle name. My dad's is Wally, which makes me laugh every time I think about it.

It looked as if Sammie's registration details were as bad as her mother's time-keeping. There were crossings out and added notes all over the place and there wasn't enough space for everything. From the look of it, Mrs Wesley had changed jobs about three times this year and every time the new contact numbers had been put in, the old ones had been roughly crossed out in Mrs Fryston's awful handwriting. No wonder Mum was in a flap if all the sheets were this messy.

Back on the computer, the cursor was flashing temptingly on the space left for Sammie's mum's latest emergency contact telephone number. I glanced at the original sheet and quickly filled it in, guessing one of the digits was a five, though it could have been an eight.

Mum ought to let me do these, I thought, I'd have them done in no time. I replaced Sammie's sheet and saw mine was next on the pile. Now that was novel, seeing my own name printed there. I suppose I thought because I went to After School club as Mum's daughter, not really as one of *them*, I would not have one.

I went to the open door and listened for a second. Mum was still counselling Jeff downstairs, so I knew I had tonnes of time. 'Of course you're concerned about her—it's only natural,' she was saying. Yuck. I began to read.

There was nothing I didn't know until I flipped over to the other side and saw some additional notes pencilled in by Jan This. 'Problems mixing,' it said. I frowned. Problems mixing what? I frowned again. 'V. clingy to A.M. (mother & playleader). Can be antagonistic, especially towards younger ones if they invade "her" space, making her unpopular.' Then underlined it said—'monitor'.

There was worse to come. Beneath that was another pencilled note that read: 'I agree—A.M.' A.M. for Ann McCormack—my own mother.

I lifted the dictionary down and looked up 'antagonistic' and that said 'a person opposed to or in competition with another' so that was a load of rubbish for a start because I never went in for competitions. Then I looked up 'monitor' and that had loads of definitions, including 'large, flesh-eating lizards', but the one that fitted was 'to check or supervise'.

The anger I had felt in the kitchen over Brandon's picture was nothing to how I felt now. I might have guessed Fanny Fryston had it in for me but for Mum

36

to write 'I agree'—that was IT. They could both get bent.

I took my registration form and fed it slowly and deliberately into Dad's paper shredder, breathing short, rapid breaths through my nose. I was so angry I felt as if my brain was on fire. Then I took the next one on the pile—Lloyd's—and did the same to his. Problems mixing? Mix this, you big losers, I fumed. I reached out for the next sheet, not even bothering to see who that belonged to and shredded that. Unpopular? Thanks a lot! That was the worst. That meant *nobody* liked you. I didn't need a dictionary to tell me that.

I would have shredded every last single one of those registration forms if I hadn't turned to see Daniel staring at me. It was only a photograph on the shelf but it was one of those portraits taken by professional photographers in supermarkets. Every feature seemed magnified and gloating, especially those annoying wide, blue eyes of his. Without thinking twice, I lined that up for the shredder, too, but the card was too thick and wouldn't go down, though it did mangle the frame a bit at the bottom. I threw it back in its place and stomped out.

Chapter Seven

Nobody said anything about the damaged photo or the missing registration forms until Saturday night when Mum came into the living room looking puzzled. 'Everything all right?' Dad asked. I watched intently, my mouth suddenly as dry as sun-bleached sand.

'What?' she said distractedly, pushing her hair back from her pale, drawn face. 'Oh, yes—it's just a couple of registration forms are missing. It's a nuisance because I'd have finished the lot otherwise.'

'Whose are missing?' I asked innocently.

'Well, funnily enough, yours and Lloyd Fountain's and Sam Riley's.'

'Oh, that is funny,' I said.

Dad got up from his armchair and gave Mum a quick embrace. 'Well, that's a lucky break then—

you'll be seeing Tanis tomorrow at chapel and I think I can help you with that Alex McCormack one. Age nine going on nineteen, lives upstairs, allergic to washing up but makes an excellent pot of tea. Sings like an angel.' He winked at me.

'Yes,' Mum said and smiled at me too. 'She does make an excellent pot of tea.'

That night, when I kissed Daniel's ashes goodnight, 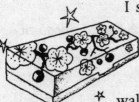 I sent him a message telepathically. 'She never even noticed you got crumpled, Danny Boy.'

Next morning Mum and I walked across to Zetland Avenue Methodist Chapel, as we did every Sunday. Caitlin was still in bed and Dad was reading the papers. They only come if there's something special on, like me singing a solo or whatever.

Mum seemed quite happy as we were getting ready to set off and I was beginning to feel bad about the forms. If Mum said anything nice to me, I decided, I would own up, but as I was zipping up my hoodie, she scowled. 'Not that silly top, Alex, please,' she sighed. *Not that silly top Alex please* didn't count as nice in my book, especially from someone wearing black tights with white sandals, so we walked to church without speaking and I kept my secret to myself.

At least Lloyd's mum was more positive about my top. She likes to stand at the door and greet us when we arrive. 'I do like your slogans, Alex,' she said. 'I haven't seen you in that one before. "Talk to the Hand". Ha! Is that the same as talking to the wall? I seem to do that a lot in my house!'

'I don't know,' I said, beaming at her, 'I suppose so.'

'Where do you want this, Tanis?' Mum asked. Mrs Fountain smiled at Mum then peered into the carrier bag she was carrying for me. 'Oh—is this your Easter Garden, Alex? It's fantastic—I love that grass! And those crosses—so upright and regal.'

Dad had superglued the crosses for me last night so I felt quite proud of my garden now.

'Thank you very much,' I replied politely. Mum hadn't even commented on it at all, apart from saying it was an awkward shape to carry.

The garden was handed over to be put on display and Mum said she'd see me later and went round to the front door of the chapel to sit in the congregation while I lined up behind Lloyd and the rest of the Sunday School kids. Lloyd turned round and gave me a fruit pastille. I swapped it with one of my jelly babies. We always swap sweets and knock out together at chapel but don't speak much at After School club. It's just the way it is. I think I feel more comfortable talking to him here—there it seems funny.

A few minutes later we trooped across the yard from the small hall where we gather to the chapel. It was Palm Sunday, so we were given palm crosses and banana plant leaves to wave around for special effect during our hymns, 'Ride on, Ride on in Majesty' and 'Jesus Rode a Donkey into Town'.

I forgot about everything when I sang. I always do. It is as if I go into another world. Today I forgot about the nasty things Mrs Fryston had written about me and how Mum had agreed. I forgot about shredding the registration forms. I forgot I was unpopular. I faced the congregation and sang my heart out.

'I wish I could sing like you, Ally,' Lloyd said at the end of the service. He always calls me Ally for some reason. 'I sound like a parrot being choked to death.'

'Yeah, you do,' I agreed as we trudged back over to the small hall for refreshments.

There, Lloyd and I took a plastic cup of squash each and a handful of biscuits and went to look at the Easter Gardens. Lloyd's was two down from mine.

'Who's done that to it?' I asked worriedly. 'I could help you fix it, if you like.'

Lloyd peered closer at the lopsided twigs and lumpy, grey mound that had collapsed on one side. 'Nope,' he said, 'that's how I left it.'

'You could have put a bit of effort in!'

'Mum thought it showed initiative,' he grinned.

'Blimey! Has she had her eyes checked recently?'

We automatically glanced across the room to where our mums were huddled over a refectory table. Mrs Fountain had Lloyd's little sister, Edith, balanced on one hip and was nodding at something Mum was saying.

'What are they doing?' Lloyd asked.

I explained about the missing registration form. 'Oh,' he said, losing interest, but once I had mentioned it, everything came flooding back and I found it hard to concentrate on the rest of the Easter Gardens. Lloyd nudged my arm at one that was even worse than his—an egg box with three matchsticks stuck in the middle. 'That's either the worst thing I've ever seen in my life or pure genius,' he whispered.

'It's the worst thing—trust me,' I told him.

He shrugged and moved along.

'Lloyd?'

'Yup?'

'You know at After School club?'

'Yup.'

'Who would you say was the most popular?'

He didn't hesitate. 'Easy. Brody. Everyone likes Brody and Brody likes everyone back.'

I couldn't argue with that. A fact's a fact.

'What about . . .' I paused, unsure whether I should go on, but I knew Lloyd. I trusted him. 'What about the most unpopular?'

Again, he didn't hesitate. 'Reggie. Definitely Reggie.'

That came as a surprise. 'Reggie?'

'Well, he was definitely the most unpopular where I was sitting on Friday. He'd had beans for breakfast and beans for lunch and you know what that means with Reggie. Trump, trump, trump all afternoon. Brody put a peg on her nose in the end. It left a red mark shaped like a sparrow's beak.'

'If you were being serious, though, Lloyd . . . who's really the most unpopular?'

'I don't know. I've never thought about it.'

I took a deep breath. 'Do you think it's me?'

He frowned and swallowed the rest of his biscuit. 'You? No, I wouldn't say that. You are different there, though.'

'How do you mean?'

'You're not the same as you are here. You can be a bit . . .'

'A bit what?'

He looked me straight in the eye. 'A bit snappy. Like you don't want anyone to talk to you so you snap to make them go away.'

'Oh!' I said. I felt hurt that Lloyd thought that.

'But you could work on it,' Lloyd added helpfully, seeing my face fall.

The word was still repeating in my head that night as I brushed my teeth before going to bed. What nobody seemed to get, I frothed at the cabinet mirror, was that I was only there because of Mum and sometimes I did have to tell people off round the craft table to help her out. They'd take advantage of her soft nature otherwise and mess about and pinch stuff. That wasn't being snappy, that was being responsible.

I dropped my toothbrush next to Caitlin's and wiped my mouth on the flannel. I decided Lloyd was a nice boy but had got it wrong and so had Mrs

Fryston. Very wrong. I wasn't snappy or unpopular or clingy or antagonistic. 'So back at you all!' I said out loud.

My mouth curved into a smile as an idea formed in my head. Back at you all was a genius idea!

Chapter Eight

Monday: the first day of the Easter holidays and the first of nine full days at After School club and the perfect opportunity to put Plan *Back at You* into action.

Mum and I were the first to arrive and the mobile felt cold, despite the warm April sun streaming through the windows. I rushed to turn the heating on, even though part of the plan was not to do any chores. A few minutes later Mrs Fryston arrived but she was with Mr Sharkey and spent ages chatting to him on the steps outside. When I pointed it out, Mum said it was because they were discussing plans for the new all-weather play surface. As if.

Meanwhile, Mum was trying to set up her craft table. She looked tired and yawned as she fumbled about on the paint trolley for scissors and card. Eight o'clock is early for someone not used to starting work until after three. 'Alex, have you seen the yellow tissue paper anywhere? I'm sure I put it out here on Friday,' she asked.

'It's next to the pipe cleaners,' I pointed out.

She drifted over to the flat packs of paper and placed them next to a pile of empty egg cartons. 'Tissue paper's lovely, isn't it? I like the sound it makes when you scrunch it up, don't you?'

I put my plan into action immediately. 'Oh, I agree,' I said, nodding.

Mum carried on chatting—even when she's tired she's enthusiastic about her craft ideas. 'I'm doing three-dimensional Easter daffodil cards this morning, though I suppose I'd better call them spring cards, hadn't I? Don't want to go upsetting anyone.'

'I agree,' I replied.

She began to pour herself a cup of coffee from the flask she always brought. 'Can you check if there are any bottles of orange poster paint left?'

'There aren't,' I said, quickly checking the bottom shelf of the trolley that had every colour but.

Mum glanced across to the door, where Mrs Fryston was now chatting to the first arrivals, a couple of new faces from Year Two and Three with their childminder. Mr Sharkey seemed to have disappeared.

'Oh, dear, they're coming in already,' Mum said, and poured her coffee back into her flask. Hot drink near five year olds is a disaster waiting to happen, she reckons. 'Alex, can you mix me some orange paint up using the red and yellow while I trim the card?' she sighed.

Ha! Just the wording I had been waiting for, Mrs McCormack. 'No, I'm ever so sorry but I can't,' I said, 'I'm not very good at mixing—it makes me antagonistic.'

Mum looked up at me quizzically. 'Don't be silly, Alex, there isn't time to mess about. Go easy on the red.'

I shook my head. 'I'm sorry, Mrs McCormack, I can't help you today. I'm not feeling very crafty. I think I'll go and read a book for a while.'

'Oh,' Mum said, a little surprised, 'OK, then.'

I sat in the book corner and waited and watched. It was quite interesting seeing things from the book corner for a change because I could see right into the cloakroom area. The older ones, like Brody and Reggie, arrived by themselves, dropped their stuff off and headed straight for their usual activity without  any fuss. Most of the younger ones were sorted out by their parents or helpers, who came in with them and had a quick word with Mrs Fryston before they left. Brandon's mum looked cross and almost shook him out of his duffel coat. She didn't kiss him goodbye or have a quick word with Jan This before she hurried off. I bet she found the little tyke as annoying as I did; I *knew* it wasn't just me. Sammie arrived late yet stayed in the cloakroom the longest. One of her big sisters—Gemma, I think— had arrived with her and there'd been a tussle over something in Sammie's bag. In the end Gemma had gone off in a huff and Sammie stuck her middle finger up at her through the glass. Lucky for her nobody saw or she would have been in big trouble.

All in all my book corner experience was quite interesting and I might do it again in future.

Eventually, Mrs Fryston gathered everyone together and reeled off the choices for the day. 'We have,' Mrs Fryston told everyone, 'spring cards with Mrs McCormack, Quick Cricket outside with Denise, chocolate nests with me, and any of the usual After School club activities that are out. Pop Kids will start tomorrow afternoon when Mrs Riley will be bringing in the karaoke machine to set us off. Right, then,' Mrs Fryston beamed, 'let's get to it!'

Yes, let's, I thought as I approached her corner.

Chapter Nine

'Hello, Alex,' Mrs Fryston said, rolling up the sleeves of her ZAPS sweatshirt as I approached, 'does your mum need something before I start?'

'I don't know, I haven't asked her,' I shrugged, pulling out a chair and sitting down between Sammie and Tasmim.

'Oh,' Mrs Fryston said, realizing I wanted to join in, 'you've come to make a chocolate nest?'

'Yup,' I said, smiling sweetly.

'Well, you're more than welcome.'

'Thank you.'

Chocolate nests were not very challenging to make, especially when we weren't allowed to heat anything ourselves. All we were meant to do was wait until Mrs Fryston poured us each a dollop of melted cooking chocolate into a titchy bowl half filled with Shredded Wheat and stir it together, pour it into a couple of bun cases and stick a mini egg or two in the middle once it has set. It should have taken about three seconds, had I not been in a chatty mood.

'It's very *clingy*, isn't it, chocolate?' I said to Mrs Fryston.

'It can be if you're not quick with it,' she confirmed, then told Tasmim not to lick the bowl out. I glanced for a second at the dark-haired Tasmim, who was small like her mother and hardly ever spoke, before continuing, 'And hard to mix. I am *so* having problems mixing,' I said.

'Are you, Alex?' the supervisor asked, puzzled, as I pretended to find the wooden spoon very awkward and 'accidentally' flicked some Shredded Wheat onto the table. 'Oh, yes, mixing is a real problem of mine. I'm just terrible at it.'

'Just stir it fast,' Sammie said helpfully, 'you have to stir it fast when you're baking in our house or everyone nicks it before you've finished. I made a recipe for lemon buns once, right, and it was supposed to make twenty-four but by the time my mam and our Gemma and our Sasha had gone past there was only enough for six!'

'Was there?' I said. 'Can I come round to your house and watch next time? I'd like to monitor that.'

'Would you?' Sammie asked uncertainly, pushing her headband away from her forehead and leaving a brown fingerprint in the middle of it.

'Definitely. Or would that make me unpopular?'

'No—'cept if you ate all the mixture and all,' Sammie replied.

'OK everyone,' Mrs Fryston instructed, 'the next step is to put a big spoonful of the mixture into your bun cases like this . . .' She broke off to demonstrate. 'And then carefully drop one or two mini eggs on top like this.' Two speckled sugar eggs, one pink, one blue, were dropped perfectly into the middle of the setting chocolate. I have to admit Jan This had made a good job of it.

'When can we eat them?' Sammie asked eagerly.

Mrs Fryston wiped her hands on a tea towel. 'I think it would be a good idea if you saved them until you got home, don't you? Show your mum what you've been up to?'

The look on Sammie's face said 'no' in capital letters but she didn't say anything.

'And make sure you all write your names on a piece of paper and put them next to your nests so nobody takes yours home by mistake,' Mrs Fryston added.

'Are you going to put "Sammie" or "Samantha Louise"?' I asked Sammie, remembering her form.

'Sammie,' she frowned. 'How did you know my middle name? I never tell nobody it.'

'Oh,' I shrugged, 'you pick up things . . .'

'I've never even told Sam,' she muttered, glancing across at Sam Riley, her best friend, who was playing Jenga with Brandon.

'Are you feeling all right, Alex?' Mrs Fryston asked.

'I'm fine, Mrs Fryston,' I said, dropping three mini eggs into my nest and squashing them down hard with my thumb. 'I'm just dandy.'

Chapter Ten

By mid-afternoon, I had run out of activities. As well as making the chocolate nests, I had played Quick Cricket, read two books, and sorted the dressing-up box into day-wear and evening-wear. Nobody could accuse me of not mixing today, I thought sourly, but I was disappointed that my 'Back at You' plan wasn't working that well. I had used every key word on my registration form and neither Mrs Fryston nor Mum had batted an eyelid.

It seemed to me that people said things or wrote things and then forgot about them, so whether I did anything good or anything bad didn't make any difference. Nobody noticed one way or the other.

Feeling miserable and a bit deflated, I headed for the only thing left to go on apart from making spring cards—the computers.

For once, the 'it-team'—Brody, Reggie, and Lloyd —were not actually on the computers but draped over a table nearby, with Reggie and Brody on one side and Lloyd opposite. They looked quite intimidating and I had to take a few quick breaths as I approached. Reggie and Brody were the most popular kids in Year Six, after all, not just here at After School club. I was only a Year Four, remember.

'Hey,' I said as I passed and slid onto a vacant computer chair.

'Hi, Alex,' Brody replied, 'what's new?'

I switched on the computer and waited for it to load. 'Nothing much,' I mumbled, searching for the games section on the desktop icon.

'We're just planning what to do for Pop Kids,' Brody continued.

'Oh.'

'I'm doing Elvis,' Reggie announced. 'You can't beat the

classics. Question is, how to put on twenty stone before next Friday.'

'I'm still torn between Kylie and Cindi Lauper,' Brody said, her voice troubled as if this was a real problem to her.

'Cindi who?' Lloyd asked.

'Lauper. I didn't know her either but my dad has these neat shots of her from the nineteen eighties. She was an American singer and wore these really cool dresses and had wild hair—Mom says she can easily fix me up with something similar.'

I felt a stab of envy as I loaded a CD into the disk drive. If my mum fixed me up I'd end up going as someone in the Salvation Army band.

'What about you, Lloydy?' Reggie asked.

'I don't know. Anyone who can't sing, I suppose,' he sighed, and I could feel his eyes drilling into my back as if wanting me to agree with him but I remembered what he had said about me yesterday and didn't turn round.

'I guess I'll definitely do Cindi,' Brody continued. 'I think Sammie's doing Kylie and I don't want to cramp her style.'

'What about you, Alex, who are you doing?' Reggie asked.

'Nobody,' I said, 'I'm just going to watch.'

'Why?'

'Just because,' I said, but I said it lightly so I wouldn't sound snappy.

The truth was I did not come from a pop music loving family and prancing around in silly clothes singing stuff about being broken hearted is not my idea of fun. I would rather make chocolate nests for two weeks.

I threw a quick glance towards the craft table. Mum had several customers, mainly little ones, all gluing and sticking. She seemed quite happy, sitting among them, passing them things and helping with the cutting. She wasn't missing me at all—probably hadn't even noticed I'd gone.

'I think I'll go on the computer,' Brody said, scraping back a chair noisily and coming to sit alongside me.

'Check out my e-mails,' Reggie told her, 'and if I've got one from someone called Fatmuddyboy, delete it quick. He's a freak—he eats live goldfish!'

Brody reached over and touched me lightly on my arm. 'You've got three new messages, by the way, if you're going on the e-pals website.'

'Three?'

'Aha. Two from Courtney again then one from Jolene. Didn't tell you in case you weren't interested.'

'You're right, I'm not,' I told her, 'you can delete mine, too.' But as soon as I had said it, I wished I hadn't. If there was one person in this world who understood me, it was Jolene. If she had been here, she'd have been with me all the way today. She would have *got* it.

I glanced across at Brody, to see what she was doing, but her long hair blocked my view until she suddenly glanced back at me, and smiled. That stopped me missing Jolene straight away. Brody's veneered front tooth was good, but not good enough to prevent it looking slightly different from the real thing. Again I saw Jolene's face full of rage and heard Brody's scream as she fell.

'Are you sure?' Brody asked, her finger hovering over the keyboard.

'I'm sure,' I said, shuddering.

Chapter Eleven

At least the next day I didn't have to do any of that mixing business or worry about unwanted e-mails. It was the start of the Pop Kids theme that meant all sit together and listen to instructions, boys and girls. Yuck. Yuck. Yuckity-yuck.

My heart sank as Brody handed round letters outlining the schedule for the next two weeks while we waited for Mrs Riley to plug all her cables into the right holes of the karaoke machine.

Pop Kids
Week One
Tuesday and Wednesday: Practise singing with
the stars on the karaoke machine
Thursday, Friday: choose your artist, plan your
outfit, learn the lyrics
Week Two
(not Monday—closed for Bank Holiday)
Tuesday: Luke and Tim with drums, guitars,
etc. (and rest of week—bring ear plugs!)
Wednesday: rehearsals and hair and make-up
tips with Kiersten Tor
Thursday: dress rehearsal & choreography
Friday: showtime! Performance at 4.00p.m.

'Who are Luke and Tim?' Lloyd asked from over
my shoulder.

'Sam Riley's big brothers—they're in a band,' I told
him dully, folding the sheet of paper and sliding it
under Tasmim's shoe in front of me.

'Oh. What is it called?' Lloyd asked, taking the
sheet back and rolling his eyes at me in disapproval.

'I don't know.'

'Huw's in a band. They're called the Hairy Pants,'

Lloyd whispered loudly as Mrs Riley fed the last cable into the machine and had a quick twiddle of the knobs before explaining how the karaoke worked.

Huw was Lloyd's older brother. He had an even older one called Calum but he was at university somewhere in Wales. 'I chose the name for them,' Lloyd told me proudly.

'Shh!' I said. 'Mrs Riley's ready.'

'Oh, all right. Keep your hairy pants on.'

Mrs Riley swept her eyes round the room to check out we were all listening then began. 'Now the idea of this is to get you used to timing your singing and being in front of an audience,' she told everyone, 'just follow the white ball on the television screen and let rip! It's great fun. Who'd like to be first?'

Sammie's arm shot into the air together with a loud 'ooh-ooh-ooh' sound that convinced Mrs Riley to give in to her straightaway. I'd have made her wait, myself. Anyway, Sammie leaped onto the stage blocks we had borrowed from the school hall and took the microphone then stared at it worriedly. 'Anything wrong, Sammie?' Mrs Riley asked.

'It's a bit smaller than our Gemma's hairbrush, that's all,' Sammie replied. 'I've been practising all weekend with it.'

That explained the tussle in the cloakrooms yesterday, I thought.

'I still don't know what I'm going to do, do you?' Lloyd whispered.

'I keep telling you—nothing.'

'Still? But why?' Lloyd asked, jamming his fingers in his ears as Sammie started belting out something about mountains not being high enough.

'I just don't want to.'

'I do,' he said, 'and I can't sing for toffee.'

To prove it, he put his hand up to be next when Sammie had finished. Now Sammie had been bad but Lloyd—Lloyd was chronic, as I knew from chapel. He was out of tune and at least three lines behind the words on the screen but he grinned all the way through it and everyone clapped like mad at the end, despite laughing their heads off at him.

Brody was up next, complete with so many fancy dance moves I knew Sammie wasn't the only one who had been practising over the weekend. Then Reggie had his go. He had the mike in one hand and a bag of doughnuts in the other. 'I'm going to be the King—

got to look the part,' he explained, spraying sugar everywhere.

'Does he mean Elvis or Henry the Eighth?' Lloyd asked.

After that it was the smaller ones and the performances got worse and worse but nobody seemed to mind. I shook my head when Mrs Riley asked me if I wanted a turn and I'm glad to say she didn't keep on about it when I said no. Instead, Mr Sharkey, who had dropped by for one of his 'quick words' with Mrs Fryston, put his hand up. 'Me! Me! Me!' he joked. Everyone moved out of the way as he shimmied forward. 'What shall I sing?' he asked, flicking through the songbook.

'"You're the Devil in Disguise"!' Reggie shouted out, quick as a flash.

Even I laughed at that one.

I still thought Pop Kids was a daft idea, though.

Chapter Twelve

I hadn't enjoyed my day and wanted to get home as quickly as possible but Mrs Wesley was doing one of her usuals and had not turned up. 'Did she say she might be late?' Mrs Fryston asked, keeping her voice level but glancing at her watch.

'No,' Sammie mumbled.

'I'll give her a call. Has she got her mobile with her, do you know?'

'Doubt it,' Sammie said. 'She chucked it across the room this morning cos it had run out of credit.'

'I'll try her work number then. It's just I've got to be out by seven and I won't have time to make myself look beautiful at this rate!' Mrs Fryston said, pretending it didn't matter really when everyone could tell it did.

'Sorry,' Sammie said, twirling her hairbrush round and round in her hand and looking miserable.

'Don't worry,' Mrs Fryston said sympathetically, ruffling Sammie's hair.

Meanwhile, I just sat on the wicker basket full of dressing-up clothes, listening to my tummy rumbling, feeling bored stiff. Mum was still faffing about with her glue pots, setting up for the next morning, when Mrs Fryston called out to her. 'Ann, is this contact number for Mrs Wesley the up-to-date one? I can't remember if it was Sam's or Sammie's you hadn't finished yet?'

Mum looked up and told her Sammie's was accurate. Mrs Fryston shook her head as if she couldn't understand. 'I'll try again,' she said and frowned and apologized when the person on the other end answered. 'Wrong number,' she said, 'unless your mum's in the maternity ward at Pinfields General, Sammie!'

'She'd better not be,' Sammie grunted.

'The five might be an eight,' I said, just wanting to get home. 'I wasn't sure when I typed it in.'

'Oh,' Mrs Fryston said shortly, shooting me a quizzical look and beginning to redial just as Mrs

Wesley came bursting through the door, full of apologies and excuses. 'Traffic's crackers tonight—road works everywhere,' she puffed. Road works? Huh! She hadn't used that one for a few weeks.

Mrs Fryston smiled tightly, said it didn't matter, and asked her to double-check her number before she left.

'Can we go now?' I said to Mum grumpily.

'Just a minute, Alex,' Mrs Fryston said when Sammie and her mum closed the door behind them, and asked me what I meant by 'typing it in'. I shrugged and explained what I had done, not really thinking much of it, to be honest. Mrs Fryston frowned. 'So that's how you knew about Sammie's middle name yesterday. I thought it seemed odd.'

Oh, trust her to hear that part and not one of my 'Back at You' words. She then turned to Mum and said in a bit of a snooty voice. 'Ann? You do know the records are confidential?'

Mum nodded and went slightly pink. That got me annoyed. Jan This had no right to tell my mum off. That was my job.

'It's not her fault if you give her too much to do. In case you didn't know, she's rubbish at typing, those records took her all week!' I stated angrily.

Mrs Fryston looked at me but before she could say anything, Mum butted in. 'Alex, don't be rude,' she whispered.

'I'm not being!' I fumed.

Mrs Fryston shook her head at me, then glanced at her watch. 'We'll need to talk about this later, Ann. I have to lock up.'

'I'm sorry, Jan,' Mum grovelled.

'Why are you apologizing to her? She should be apologizing to you,' I muttered loudly. 'You do all the work while she just chats to her boyfriend all day.'

'Off you go now, Alex,' Mrs Fryston said calmly but firmly, 'quickly.'

Chapter Thirteen

'How could you talk to Jan like that?' Mum asked as
we waited at the pelican crossing. 'Whatever were
you thinking? You were so rude.'

'She was rude to me!' I answered.

'I've never felt so ashamed,' she sniffed.

I glanced up at her to see if she was going to start
crying in public, because if she did I was legging it
home ahead of her. She was so embarrassing at times.
'I don't know why I'm getting all the blame. I was
only sticking up for you,' I told her. 'You know you're
not fast at typing. And you were the one who told me
to do it anyway.'

'I asked you to save the work, that's all,' Mum
mumbled, 'you know that.'

'Green man,' I said.

'What?'

'Green man! We can cross.'

She seemed so distracted I had to pull her across the road. Even outside the house she couldn't get her act together and fumbled for ages trying to unlock the door. 'Look at me,' she said, 'I'm so upset I can't even get into my own home.'

I pushed past her and into the hallway where I flung down my bag and coat and twizzled round. 'I don't see what all the fuss is about! It was only one little digit. And Sammie's mum is always late and you and Mrs Fryston are always moaning about it so don't pretend you're not because . . .'

Mum didn't let me finish. Her finger shook as she pointed it towards the stairs.

'Go to your room now and stay there until I tell you to come down,' she croaked.

Her chin wobbled as I decided whether to take any notice of her or not. 'Don't worry, I will!' I said in the end, seeing as I had to get changed anyway.

I cleared the stairs two at a time and gave my

bedroom door a mighty bang as I slammed it behind me. I waited for a few seconds, expecting Caitlin to come running out from next door wondering what was the matter. That would have been good because Caitlin would have listened and felt sorry for me and been on my side, but everything stayed eerily quiet and I remembered it was Tuesday and band practice.

I sat on my bed and stared at my trainers. I stared and stared and waited and waited but nothing happened. Mum didn't come up to apologize and tell me there was a cup of tea and a sandwich ready downstairs. She didn't even come to say I'd done wrong and don't do it again but there was a cup of tea and a sandwich ready downstairs. She didn't come at all.

After a while I got so bored I trundled downstairs and into the kitchen where I could smell something cooking.

'What's for dinner?' I asked. 'If it's chicken I'll—'

'Alex,' Mum said in a low, gruff voice, 'I thought I told you to stay upstairs.'

'I did.'

'Go back until I tell you to come down.'

'I don't want to.'

She dropped the wooden spoon she had been stirring with onto the hob where it splattered red sauce everywhere. 'Alex, go to your room!' she screamed.

I stared at her in amazement and opened my mouth to speak but she then picked up the spoon and threw it right across the kitchen where it bounced off a wall cabinet and landed on the quarry tiles with a clatter. 'Now!' she screeched.

I turned and fled.

It seemed a long, long time until I heard voices downstairs and finally Dad knocked on my door and said, 'Alex, it's me' and entered, all long-faced and serious. 'Oh dear, Alex,' he said, 'what happened? Your mum's really upset down there.'

'And I'm really upset up here!' I sniffed, blowing my nose into a tissue and adding it to the pile of others in the bin. 'Mum shouted at me and threw a spoon.'

'Tell me what happened,' he said and sat on the bed beside me, stroking my hair. 'And were you really rude to Mrs Fryston?' he asked after I had told him my version.

'Yes,' I admitted.

He sighed heavily. 'Oh, Alex,' he said and now that I had replayed the scene again out loud, even my version made me sound pretty bad. I knew I shouldn't have said that about Mr Sharkey. I liked him a lot and hoped Mrs Fryston didn't tell him what I said.

My shoulders began to judder and I began crying again. 'I don't know w . . . w . . . why everyone's making s . . . such a fuss over a silly telephone number,' I stuttered. 'There was no need for M . . . Mum to sh . . . shout at me. She knows very w . . . well I disapprove of sh . . . shouting!'

'Maybe next time you'll do as you're told the first time and there'll be no need for anyone to shout at you,' Dad pointed out.

'But M . . . Mum never shouts at me, no m . . . matter what I s . . . say,' I wailed.

'I know,' he said quietly, 'she's gone too far the other way.'

'What's that m . . . mean?'

He shook his head. 'Oh, nothing. Look, I'm going to get changed. Caitlin's coming up in a minute with something on a tray for you . . .'

'That's all right—I'll eat d . . . downstairs,' I said, jumping up, 'and I'll s . . . say s . . . sorry to Mum, I suppose.'

'No,' Dad said, shaking his head again and putting an arm out to steady me, 'eat in here then go to bed. It's best if you stay out of the way a while until Mum calms down.'

I didn't understand. 'But I n . . . never eat in my r . . . room—Mum always tells me we'll g . . . get mice,' I pointed out.

Dad cleared his throat. 'Well, we'll risk it, just this one time, eh? Anyway, the good news is, you can have a lie-in tomorrow!'

'What do you m . . . mean?' I hiccuped.

'You can skip After School club for a day and spend it with Caitlin.'

'Why?'

Dad patted me on the knees. 'It's probably best to let your mother sort things out with Mrs Fryston on her own.'

'OK,' I shrugged. I didn't fancy seeing Mrs Fryston again so soon anyway, especially the more I thought about my parting comment and her face after I had said it.

Then I realized something else. 'What, s . . . so I don't even have to c . . . come downstairs to k . . . kiss Daniel goodnight?'

Dad, thinking it worried me,

75

said no, but I could give him two kisses tomorrow night if I wanted. That really brought home how serious everyone was being and I didn't like it. My stomach, which had been rumbling with hunger, stopped immediately, as if it had been switched off, leaving me with a nasty queasy feeling instead. 'Tell Caitlin not to bring the tray—I think I'll just go straight to bed,' I said, my voice steadier now but so hushed Dad probably hardly heard it.

'OK,' Dad said and kissed me lightly on the top of my head. 'It's hard being nine, isn't it? There's so much to learn.'

'I've d . . . done all my homework,' I reassured him, hiccuping again from crying so much.

'That's not what I meant,' he said and left the room quietly.

A few minutes later Caitlin peered in and whispered my name but I pretended to be asleep and didn't answer.

Chapter Fourteen

I woke up the next morning at my usual time and was about to leap out of bed until everything came flooding back. I glanced at my alarm clock and knew Mum would still be downstairs and I didn't want to go down to face her. Even though I had said I would apologize, part of me still felt yesterday's mess hadn't been all my fault, especially when I thought about her throwing that spoon . . .

So I waited until I heard the door bang before I got up. I knew Caitlin was in bed but I still felt alone as I walked slowly past her bedroom and down the stairs into the kitchen. There was such a gloomy feeling to the house. The only signs of Mum having been here a few minutes earlier were a scattering of crumbs on the worktop from where she had prepared her sandwiches.

I don't care, I told myself at first. Ask me if I'm bothered about not going to stupid After School club? *Ask me if I'm bothered.* That's what Jolene used to say to people when they annoyed her. Jolene. Was I as naughty as her? No way. I hadn't broken anyone's tooth. I'd just been a bit cheeky, that's all.

I made myself a slice of toast and planned out my day—it was going to be good. I had the freedom to do whatever I wanted without anybody breathing down my neck. The trouble was, by half past nine I had finished doing everything I could think of—I'd had breakfast, read, watched TV, sketched, sharpened every coloured pencil I had, and tested all my felt pens to throw away ones that didn't work. Now what? I ended up watching a chat show about men cheating on their partners. It wasn't very interesting. I prefer it when they do make-overs for ugly people.

Finally Caitlin awoke and I flung my arms round her in relief as she sloped into the kitchen for her breakfast at eleven o'clock. 'Hurray—you're up!' I announced.

'I know—"put out the flags". I've heard it all before

from Dad,' she yawned as she poured herself a bowl of muesli.

'I mean it—I've been so bored. Can we do something? Go to the pictures?' I asked as she slid on to the tall stool opposite me at the breakfast bar. 'Or maybe bowling?'

She pulled a mardy face. 'You are joking, right? In case you've forgotten, you've been grounded, sister. No treats, by order of the management,' Caitlin replied, looking at me steadily and added, 'I hope you are taking this seriously, Alex.'

'I am!'

She peered at me, looking for signs. 'You'd better be! I know it's a novelty for you that they're actually following through with a punishment but I've not seen Mum as wound up as she was last night—not for a long time.'

'Well, she shouted at me!' I said in my defence. 'And she threw a spoon.'

'Huh! Is that all? Just be grateful it's not like the olden days,' Caitlin said unsympathetically.

'What do you mean?'

'She'd have gone up the wall, never mind the spoon.'

'Mum?'

'Yes, Mum. She used to scream her head off at the tiniest thing. Don't you remember? Dad too for that matter.'

'No.'

'You must do! Why do you think you hate scenes? Even now?'

'Oh,' I said, taking in this piece of incredible news.

But Caitlin didn't give me time to ponder. She carried straight on with her rant. 'Not that she's like that now, so you've no excuse for yesterday. You do know Mum could get the sack?'

That caught me by surprise. 'Could she?'

'Of course she could. All she needs is for a parent to complain about her allowing you to see private material and that's it. How would you like it if some kid in your class read all your personal details in Mr Sharkey's filing cabinet?'

I chose to ignore that uncomfortable idea. 'Well, I hope she does get the sack,' I replied heatedly, 'I hate After School club!'

Caitlin looked at me and frowned. 'Why? What's to hate? It sounds great to me—all those games and things.'

'That's only for the normal kids. I'm not a normal kid,' I told her.

'Course you are.'

'I'm not. I'm with Mum—that makes me different.'

'Well, it shouldn't do.'

'Well, it does and anyway, stop getting at me. I know I was a bit rude yesterday but—'

'A bit!'

'Let me finish!' I said, getting wound up. 'You weren't there, you don't know why.'

'Go on then,' she drawled, 'I'm all ears.'

'OK, well, I didn't even tell Dad this but Mrs Fryston wrote nasty, horrible things about me and I was only rude because I was cross about that,' I sniffed and felt tears spring to my eyes again.

'What nasty, horrible things?' Caitlin asked, seeming interested.

'She wrote on the back of my form that I was clingy and unpopular and antagonistic and Mum agreed with her. "I agree" she put, in capitals, too.'

Caitlin finished the last spoonful of muesli and looked directly at me. 'And are you?'

'What?'

'Clingy, unpopular, and antagonistic?'

'No.'

'Why would Jan write it, then? She always seems all right to me.'

'I don't know, do I?'

She gave me another long, searching look. 'Why else?' she asked.

'Why else what?'

'Why else do you hate After School club?' Caitlin repeated as if talking to a baby.

'Because . . .' I gulped.

'Go on,' Caitlin said but softer this time, pushing her empty bowl to one side.

'Because Mum always makes a fuss of the little ones, especially Brandon Potty-face and even if they make something rubbish she tells them it's good but when I make something . . .'

I went on and on, telling Caitlin one thing after another about After School club and she listened properly and didn't interrupt once, even to laugh because I was hiccuping through half of it and must have sounded funny.

'You're right,' Caitlin said when I had finished.

'What about?'

'All of it. Mum is like that. She spends all her time and energy giving to other people and forgets to give some to us. I bet I could walk into the house with nothing on but my trumpet on my head and she'd still not see me.'

'Exactly.'

Now we were talking.

Chapter Fifteen

I shuffled on my stool to get more comfortable. This was how it should be—sisters swapping complaints about their parents—supporting each other. Only Caitlin spoilt it almost immediately.

'But Mum can't help it,' she continued sadly, 'it's how she's survived since Daniel died. She wasn't like that before. Before he died she used to . . .'

But I was too excited to let her finish. 'I knew it! I knew it would be his fault! He ruins everything in this family!' I reached across so she could give me a high-five but she just stared at me in horror.

'What?' Caitlin asked, her face clouding over alarmingly.

'He's to blame—you just said so . . .' I said before stopping abruptly at the sight of her eyes which had turned as dark and dangerous as an abandoned well.

'Shut up, you little brat!' Caitlin hissed.

Her words pelted me like cold, hard hailstones. It was the final straw. My whole family hated me! I burst into tears and began to scramble down from the breakfast bar to escape but Caitlin caught me by the arm and held me fast, forcing me to look at her.

'Let's get one thing straight, Alex! You can't blame Daniel for *anything*. He was four years old! Do you think he caught meningitis on purpose? Do you think he thought, I know, I'll die and then everyone in the family will be really messed up? I'll put my mum on tablets for the rest of her life and make my dad work long hours so he doesn't have to come home, and I'll make Caitlin miss me so much she won't let me be buried properly?'

My head reeled from too many details.

'No, but . . .'

'No but nothing!' Caitlin shouted, suddenly letting go of my arm and pushing it away as if it was contaminated meat. 'I can't believe you think that, Alex!' Spit flew from her mouth as she yelled.

I flinched and leaned backwards. If I had thought Mum was bad yesterday, it was nothing compared to Caitlin now. She seemed so angry I was beginning to get that sick feeling I had just before Jolene lashed out at Brody. For the first time in my life, I was frightened of my sister.

Caitlin looked at me for a second then blinked. Taking a deep, steadying breath she lowered her voice from a shout to something calmer and less scary. 'It's all right, Alex—I'm sorry—I'm not going to hurt you,' she said, wiping her eyes roughly.

I bit my lip and nodded, but my heart was still hammering away. Caitlin put out her hand and covered mine with it and this time her eyes were as tearful as mine. 'I suppose it's harder for you to understand, because you never knew Daniel, but he was my little brother and I loved him to bits. I miss him every day and you'd better learn to respect that.'

I took a big risk and asked a question to something I had never understood. 'Even though it was ages ago?'

'It's not as bad now,' she admitted, 'but I still feel there's a bit missing, like a hole that can never be filled. We all do, especially Mum. It hit her the hardest.'

'Even with me around?' I asked in a small voice. 'Is there still a hole?'

She nodded. 'Even if there'd been ten of you around, Alex.'

There was a short pause and Caitlin, seeming to understand what I was feeling, added hastily, 'But that's not to say we don't love you, because we do. All of us.'

I knew she meant it, too, and that it was true but it hurt that I couldn't fill that hole. I should have been able to. After all, I had replaced him in the family, hadn't I? Nobody had to tell me I wouldn't have been born if he hadn't died. It was obvious. 'Would it have been better if I'd been a boy, like Daniel? Would there still be something missing then?' I persisted.

'It would have been worse, I think. For you especially.'

I pressed on. 'I suppose it's because I'm not sweet and perfect like him.'

Caitlin blinked. 'Sweet and perfect? What makes you think Daniel was that?'

'He was, wasn't he? Like an angel, Mum always says.'

'Was he heck!' Caitlin said, managing a watery smile. 'It's just that when someone dies, especially a child, people build up this ideal picture of them. Dan could be a little monster! He was always breaking my toys and you should have seen him if he didn't get his own way. He'd hold his breath until he went blue. Oh—he used to scare us silly sometimes.'

'Did he? Honest?'

'Honest. Early reports from his nursery school were that he was a bit of a handful.'

'Oh.'

'But he could also be the nicest boy in the world and when he laughed it filled the whole room.' Her eyes welled with tears again and Caitlin withdrew her hand and quickly took her bowl to the sink where she began splashing it in water from the tap. She let the water gush everywhere, not caring that she was getting wet.

'Caitlin?'

'Aha?' she said gruffly.

'What did you mean before—about not letting Daniel be buried?'

She didn't turn round but stared out of the kitchen window, into the back garden. 'I didn't want him to be buried. I didn't want him to be in the dark—he was scared of the dark—so Mum and Dad had him cremated. Then, when the ashes came, I didn't want them to be buried either, because it felt like the same thing, so they put him in my special box Grandad had bought me for Christmas and left him on the mantelpiece so I could see him every day.'

'I didn't know that,' I said. 'I didn't know it was your box. I thought it was Mum's idea.'

She turned to me and shook her head sorrowfully. 'No, it was mine. It all seems a bit babyish now but it helped me at the time. I was only six, remember. I suppose we just got used to having him there on the mantelpiece—we ought to move him really.'

'I suppose.'

Caitlin sniffed and wiped her eyes on her dressing gown sleeve. 'Blimey what a gloomy topic. How did we get on to this?' she asked.

'Tell me what else Daniel did,' I said, 'he sounds interesting.'

My sister's smile lit up her face as she returned to her seat. 'Oh, Alex, I've been dying for you to ask me! There was this one time, right, and Dad had these new spiked golfing shoes and Mum had these new cushions . . .'

Chapter Sixteen

As Caitlin told me about all the naughty things my brother had got up to, I found my feelings towards him changing. It was as if I had been given a new pair of eyes and ears to see and hear things differently. Everything associated with him I had hated before, seemed to have a story behind it, like the time Mum

had taken him for that photograph in the supermarket and when the photographer had asked him his name he'd said 'My name is Daniel and my willy is called Tommy Sausage'. How could I look at that picture of him again and not giggle? I didn't resent any of it now that Caitlin had helped me to see Daniel as a real person and I didn't feel jealous of him for her liking him so much because I could see why. I would have missed him, too, and stopped him from being buried in the dark if I had been around then.

I wished she had carried on with her stories but when she glanced at the clock she nearly had a heart attack. 'No! It's two o'clock! I haven't even started my English essay!'

'Or got dressed,' I pointed out.

'Teenagers, eh?' she grinned.

She reached out and gave me such a bear hug on her way out I could hardly breathe. 'You going to be OK? Do you forgive me for shouting at you?' she asked.

'I'll get over it,' I said.

'You looked so scared I felt like an axe murderer.'

'You looked like one, too,' I replied solemnly. I didn't really want to be reminded of that part of our talk but when she left I forced myself to think back to when I was little—two or three. I tried to picture Mum's angry face from yesterday then but nothing came. All I remembered was being in my bedroom a lot of the time and singing, but when I sang, I didn't feel happy, I felt anxious, and had my fingers in my ears. Sometimes I hid under my bed for some reason and Caitlin cuddled me a lot but that's about all that I could think of. Maybe I had blotted everything out. I didn't know. All I did know was I needed to show Caitlin and Dad and especially Mum how sorry I was for how I had been.

I spent late afternoon sitting hunched up on my bedroom windowsill, staring out onto Zetland Avenue, waiting for Mum to come home. I had so much I wanted to say to her I thought that I would burst. At about five o'clock her figure appeared at the pelican crossing. 'Great, she's early!' I yelped and ran downstairs.

Caitlin was in the kitchen, finishing her lunch-tea. 'Where's the fire?' she asked as I dashed past on my way to the front of the house but I didn't have time to answer.

'Mum!' I said breathlessly as I held open the door for her. 'I'm sorry about yesterday. I promise not to be rude to you or Mrs Fryston ever again. I'll . . .'

But she walked straight past, her face pale and troubled. 'Tea or coffee, Mum?' Caitlin called from the other side of the hallway.

'Coffee, please,' Mum replied in a dull monotone.

I stood nearby as she dropped her bag by the hat stand and unzipped her fleece jacket. 'I'm ready to go back to After School club tomorrow,' I gabbled, 'I'll mix and everything, I promise.'

'You can forget your empty promises,' she sighed, 'especially as neither of us is going to After School club tomorrow or the day after or the day after that.'

'Why?' I asked, then swallowed hard. 'You didn't get the sack, did you?'

I held my breath, praying she'd say no.

'Jan felt I needed a break, that's all,' Mum said, striding towards the kitchen. 'She felt working during the holidays as well as during term-time might be putting too much "strain" on me. Where she gets that idea from, I don't know, but she's the one who makes the decisions. She's the boss.'

For once I didn't leap in and take sides against Mrs Fryston. Instead I followed Mum meekly into the kitchen where Caitlin handed Mum a coffee. 'It's not a bad idea, Mum, taking a break,' Caitlin said.

'Isn't it?' Mum replied glumly.

'You can spend some quality time at home. Put your feet up.'

Mum's face registered that she hadn't got a clue what that meant. She looked so miserable and it was all my fault. I had to put it right. While Caitlin offered to make Mum a sandwich, I quietly backed out of the kitchen and headed for the front door.

Chapter Seventeen

The After School club was still busy when I burst in, all flushed from the sprint across Zetland Avenue. A few kids were in the cloakroom, packing all their things together with their parents and childminders and I had to thread my way between them to get to Mrs Fryston. Sammie and Brody, who were singing a duet in front of the full-length mirror, hairbrushes in hand, paused for a second as I barged past, then shrugged and continued their song.

I strode straight up to Mrs Fryston, who was chatting to Reggie and Lloyd by her desk. 'I'm sorry to interrupt,' I apologized as they all stared at me in surprise, 'but please don't sack my mum, Mrs Fryston —it wasn't her fault I shredded those registration forms. I was just cross and jealous because of Daniel and I took it out on Brandon and everyone else but I've got new eyes now and I'm cured. And I know Mum's not the most interesting helper but the little ones like her the best and you know that's a fact.' Then I left.

Back home, Mum and Caitlin were still in the kitchen. I heard their voices murmuring as I sneaked past and up the stairs. I sat on my bed for a while, to get my breath back. After a minute I tried reading a book to distract me but it didn't work. It had been a confusing day and it was too much to take in details of made-up lives when so much was going on in mine.

At six o'clock, I heard the doorbell ring, then Caitlin calling for me to come down. I paused for a second, my heart beating rapidly as I peered over the banisters. There in the hallway stood Mrs Fryston, and I was probably the only one who knew why she was there. 'Wish me luck,' I telegraphed silently to Daniel's picture on the wall.

'What's the matter, Jan?' Mum asked and I felt my stomach leap as Mrs Fryston stared up at me.

'I just wanted to check that Alex got home all right. I presumed she had come alone.'

'Where to?' Mum asked, confused.

'The club.'

'Have you just been there by yourself?' Caitlin demanded sharply.

'I crossed with the green man!' I muttered.

Caitlin shook her head at me but I knew I could explain everything to her later. It was Mum I needed to get through to right now. I turned to her, willing her to see I was a changed girl as Mrs Fryston repeated what I had just confessed to her in the mobile.

'I'm sorry, Jan, I had no idea she had shredded anything,' Mum apologized sorrowfully.

'It does confirm everything we discussed today, though, doesn't it?' Mrs Fryston replied mysteriously. No prizes for guessing who was the main topic of that discussion. I felt myself tense.

'Yes it does,' Mum said in a resigned way.

'But, Mum,' Caitlin said quietly, 'remember what I've just told you.'

Mum looked at Caitlin, then down at me. I stared back at her, trying not to cry, knowing she thought the same as Mrs Fryston, that I was naughty and spoilt. The words 'I agree' flashed before me and I waited for her to send me upstairs in disgrace again.

Instead, her face cleared and she slid her arm round my shoulder and pulled me close. 'Alex has been a bit unhappy lately, Jan. I'm going to have a talk to her tonight and get to the bottom of it.'

Mrs Fryston nodded and I was surprised to hear her say, 'That's good. That's what she needs.' I felt relief flow through me like a gust of warm air but Mrs Fryston had more to add. She bent down close and made me look into her eyes. 'Alex, you do know you must never, ever read After School club business?'

'Yes,' I whispered. Her breath smelt of peppermint.

'And that you have put your mother in a very awkward position?'

'Yes,' I whispered again.

'But it was brave of you to come and see me, so when we see you after the holidays, we can start again with a clean slate, can't we?'

'Yes,' I said but this time the whisper was so low I barely heard it myself.

'Why after the holidays?' Caitlin asked.

'Excuse me?' Mrs Fryston asked, straightening up.

Caitlin casually rubbed at a mark on her T-shirt.

'Well, if Alex has problems mixing at After School club, how's it going to help her by not mixing at all?'

'Well,' Mrs Fryston said, 'I just presumed with Ann taking a few days off, Alex would want to as well. I think a bit of time-out for her would be a good thing.'

'Time-out won't solve anything with Alex,' Caitlin continued, looking at me then back to Mrs Fryston, 'she needs time-in. She already sees herself as outside the group because Mum's there but if Mum's not around, it will give Alex a chance to show she *isn't* clingy and *can* mix.'

Mrs Fryston looked at Caitlin with a bemused expression on her face. 'I take it you're doing psychology as one of your A levels?' she stated.

'How can you tell?' Caitlin asked.

'I have one at home just like you!' she grinned.

Then she turned to me. 'What do you think, Alex? Could you cope with a whole day of Pop Kids and e-pals on your own?'

I looked into the eyes I usually avoided and saw how kind and patient they were. I realized Mrs Fryston was prepared to give me another chance, despite my bad attitude yesterday and all the other times.

'See you at half-eight, Mrs Fryston,' I said.

That night, Mum and Dad sat down with me and talked to me in a way they had never talked before. They answered all my questions, though sometimes it was difficult for them and Mum's eyes would flick towards the mantelpiece every time I mentioned Daniel.

'Is there anything else you'd like to ask?' Dad said eventually, glancing at his watch. It was way past my bedtime.

'No, just that Caitlin said you used to both shout a lot but I don't remember that.'

'Thanks,' Caitlin said, 'just drop me in it, why don't you?'

Dad opened his mouth to reply but it was Mum who answered first. 'Caitlin's right, we did. Dad and I were very hurt and angry when Daniel died and we wanted someone to blame so we blamed each other. We went through a very bad patch when you were a toddler.'

'I'm glad you're not any more,' I said.

'Well, we've got you to thank for that, pal,' Dad smiled and Mum nodded.

'Me? How?'

'Your singing. You'd sing to drown out our voices.

When we realized what you were doing and why, we knew it was time to do something about it and your mum and I went for counselling together. It helped a lot.'

'Oh!' I exclaimed as my memory of hiding under the bed and singing with my fingers in my ears suddenly made sense.

Dad began collecting the empty supper plates and cups. 'The voice of an angel you had—even then. Though we did get tired of "Row, row, row your boat" over and over again!'

'I'll bet,' I grinned and yawned loudly. 'I'm going to bed.'

I gave everyone an extra long hug and when I kissed Daniel, I meant it with all my heart.

Chapter Eighteen

If missing After School club had felt strange yesterday, the idea of going to After School club on my own felt even stranger, especially as Dad was taking me on the way to work. It was really odd, drawing up in the car with all the other parents dropping their kids off in theirs.

'Well, this is a novelty,' Dad said as he waited for Brody's mum's huge jeep-thing to move off so he could take her space. 'Have you got everything, Alex?'

I grabbed my sandwich box and nodded, feeling suddenly shy and apprehensive. It was like my first day at school all over again. 'Will you come in with me, Dad?' I asked him.

He checked his watch and nodded. 'Well, seeing as it's you, pal,' he said and got out of the car. I smiled at him gratefully.

We strolled round the side of school and then across the rear playground towards the mobile hut. 'So that's the famous After School club, is it?' Dad asked.

'Haven't you seen it before?'

'No—I've never needed to,' he replied.

'What do you reckon to it? Would it get a good asking price?'

'Not with that flat roof,' he said immediately.

We reached the bottom of the steps and Dad ruffled my hair. 'Good luck, Alex. Everything will be OK.'

'I know,' I said but I wasn't sure I meant it.

It wasn't easy, spending a whole day on my own at After School club. Sammie was definitely still angry with me. 'Done any more spying lately, *Mary*?' she asked when I went to buy my break-time sweets from her. I didn't ask how she had found out my middle name.

Brandon wouldn't let me be friends with him either. When I asked him if I could help him with some sticking, he had just looked at me and shaken his head. 'No thank you, you'll just spoil it, like always.'

I wanted to say, 'I'm not like that now,' but he wouldn't have understood. After those two knock-backs I didn't feel brave enough to join Reggie and the gang at the computers, so I read instead. Trouble was, I became worried Mrs Fryston might not think that counted as mixing, because I just *knew* she was watching me, so I played board games with Tasmim and a couple of new kids. It was a bit boring, if I'm honest, but not as boring as being at home would have been. Mum was using the time to catch up with all her support groups—not my idea of holiday fun.

In the afternoon, everyone was rehearsing for Pop Kids. Mrs Riley had taken the karaoke back and now CD players and DVDs sprouted up all over the place. I had only missed one day but it felt as if everything had changed without me. Sammie's hairbrush idea had caught on and everyone seemed to be singing into one in time to their chosen pop song. People were jigging about or concentrating on setting their CDs up properly. Once everyone got going the noise was terrible—I thought the mobile was going to vibrate so much its foundations would cave in.

I began to panic and looked for somewhere to hide. Reggie had taken over the library area, where I had been skulking, and had to be told several times to get off the table which he was using as a stage. 'I bet you wouldn't tell the real Elvis off if he was here,' he complained to Mrs Fryston.

Mrs Fryston folded her arms across her chest and looked up at him. 'You're right, Reggie. If Elvis were here, dancing on a craft table years after he'd died, I would not tell him off. I'd run out of the mobile screaming, seeing as I'm scared of ghosts. Now, get down, please, before you break your neck.'

'But I need the height,' Reggie complained.

'Use the stage blocks.'

'They're gay.'

'How can they be gay, you daft lad? What you mean is there's someone on them. Just ask people to move up.'

'Elvis does not share the stage with minions,' Reggie declared solemnly, clambering down from the table and walking off in a pretend-huff.

'Are you OK, Alex?' Mrs Fryston asked as I tried to sidle past.

'I'm fine,' I said over-enthusiastically.

'How's everything at home?' she asked carefully.

'OK. Caitlin's probably just getting up and Mum was going to visit the hospice.'

'That's Ann—always on the go.'

Mrs Fryston hesitated, as if she was going to say something else, then looked at me and changed the subject altogether. 'Have you decided which song you're going to sing?'

'Erm . . . not yet.'

Mrs Fryston touched me gently on the shoulder and twisted me round. 'Some people are doing duets, you know. Sam and Sammie over there . . .'

We turned to the dressing-up area where Sam and Sammie were dancing back to back, or trying to, but as Sammie towered over Sam it looked a bit strange and Sammie had to keep stopping and wagging her hairbrush because Sam's timing was all wrong. '. . . and so are Brandon and Tasmim . . .'

I found that hard to believe— Tasmim was so quiet I couldn't imagine her joining in but I was wrong. There she was swaying side-to-side with Brandon, singing along and laughing. 'That's nice,' I said.

I was rewarded with a warm smile from the supervisor. 'It is, isn't it? Actually, the only one I'm a wee bit concerned about is Lloyd. He keeps telling me he's OK but I get the feeling he's struggling a bit with his song. Maybe you could see what the problem is while I stop Elvis leaving the building?'

Over by the computers, Lloyd was sprawled out flat on his stomach, operating a cassette tape with one hand while chewing an apple held in the other. He didn't look as if he was struggling that much to me. He just looked like he always did. Like Lloyd.

Then I realized what Mrs Fryston was doing. I'd seen it a million times from the craft table. She was finding me an appropriate friend and edging me in like she did with all the new kids who seemed a bit lost. Before I'd always thought how bossy and interfering she was but now, with my new eyes, I knew it was clever of her. Sometimes kids did need a nudge in the right direction. 'I'll go help him,' I told Mrs Fryston.

'Good girl,' she smiled.

Chapter Nineteen

Lloyd was happy to let me do a duet with him because he said my voice would help drown out his. He had chosen a song called 'Wasted' by the Hairy Pants just so we could be different from everyone else. He played the tape to me a few times. It was very loud and very fast and Lloyd's idea of a dance routine to go with it was to shake our heads a lot as if we were being attacked by wasps then to stomp around in between as if we were killing them. 'It's a bit manic,' I said to Lloyd, puffed out after the first sing-through.

'Yeah,' he said happily, 'it's a blinder. Let's go through it again—after three—one . . . two . . .'

That kind of set the scene for the rest of the holidays at After School club. I joined in as many things as I could in the mornings, then practised my duet with Lloyd in the afternoons. At first, I really missed Mum, and had difficulty in stopping myself from telling Denise, who was running the craft table, that she was putting the equipment and materials back in the wrong places.

By Thursday, though, I had settled into a routine. I said goodbye to Dad, hung my jacket up, and just mucked in with everybody else. Sammie was still a bit distant with me and Brandon kept well away but I told myself I couldn't blame them and tried not to worry about it. I remembered Jolene telling me you couldn't force people to like you. 'If they do, they do, if they don't, hard cheese.' As long as Mrs Fryston knew I was keeping my promise, that was the main thing, I told myself.

Before I realized it, the holiday was nearly over and it was time for the Pop Kids to go live in front of all the parents and carers.

'You don't have to come,' I said to everyone at home the night before. 'Our song's not very good.'

'What is it?' Caitlin asked.

' "Wasted" by the Hairy Pants.'

'Sounds painful,' Dad joked.

'It is,' I said, 'and our dancing is even worse. In fact, the more I think about it, the more I definitely don't want you to come.'

Mum glanced up from her armchair. 'I've got to come—there's a staff meeting afterwards.'

'Oh,' I said. It was the first time she had mentioned After School club all week, apart from asking me if I had behaved myself the second I put my foot through the door.

'The meeting's not about me, is it?' I asked sheepishly.

'No,' Mum informed me, 'it's about the new all-weather surface.'

'Ooh, the excitement,' Caitlin teased.

'I think we've had enough excitement in the house, don't you?' Mum said pointedly then looked at me. 'What top are you wearing tomorrow?'

'The Bad Girl one—it goes with the song,' I replied.

'Oh,' she said shortly.

'I can wear something plain if you like,' I mumbled, though I didn't really want to.

'No, no,' she said in a clipped voice. 'You'd better get an early night, Alex,' she added.

I said goodnight but went to bed feeling as if I had let her down all over again. I knew how she hated my tops.

Chapter Twenty

The next morning was hectic. We all had to help turn the mobile hut into 'The ZAP Spot'—a pretend disco. While some helped Mrs Fryston and Mrs Riley put up flashing disco lights and glittery disco balls, others queued for Brody's mum, Kiersten, to put on their make-up. It took hours.

In the afternoon, because we didn't have to change into anything fussy like everyone else, I helped put chairs out for the parents and Lloyd watched Sam Riley's brothers set up their drum kit and keyboards off stage. Luke and Tim were supposed to have been backing everyone's songs all week but they'd been 'on the road' and only turned up today. Mrs Riley had been embarrassed and called them a pair of lazy articles.

I was halfway through the chairs when Lloyd came up to me, his face the colour of the grass in my Easter Garden. 'What's up?' I asked.

'The drum kit—Sam's brothers—they're The Mass.'

'Oh—so?'

'We can't do our song!'

'Why?'

'The Hairy Pants hate The Mass—they're deadly rivals. We can't do it—we can't do "Wasted".'

'Well, why can't we just not let Sam's brothers play it? We can use the tape we always use.'

Lloyd looked over his shoulder and whispered tearfully, 'Because I'm not supposed to have it—it's new material. I thought Huw wouldn't mind us airing it—for promotion purposes—but there's no way now. He'd kill me—lots of times and in many ways.'

'Now you tell me! Well, what are we going to sing then?'

'I don't know!' Lloyd squealed.

'Hurry up with the chairs, you two,' Denise called over, 'the parents are here.'

We were all hustled to the stage blocks where we

were supposed to sit in order of appearance. That meant I was on the back row with Sammie and Sam, then Brody, then me, Lloyd, and at the end Reggie, who was to be the final act. 'What are we going to do?' I asked Lloyd again in an urgent whisper. 'Mrs Fryston's going to call out our names—we can't just say—"We'll give it a miss, thanks".'

'Why not?' Lloyd replied miserably.

'Because,' I said, and stared out into the audience. Mum, Dad, and Caitlin were just taking their seats. Caitlin caught my eye and waved and I waved back shyly. I knew I had to sing. I knew it didn't matter what I sang but I had to sing something, for them. 'Listen, Lloyd,' I said to him, 'this is what we're going to do . . .'

'We can't,' he said, his face turning from artificial green to a genuine puce, 'everyone'll laugh.'

'It's either that or "Wasted",' I told him fiercely, 'and Huw's sitting right within thumping distance.'

I wasn't kidding, either. The Fountains had arrived late and had to sit right at the front. Huw, with cropped hair and dressed entirely in black, stared moodily ahead. Lloyd sank back in his chair and groaned.

'Right, everyone,' Mrs Fryston began, looking

alarming in a silver jump-suit and rainbow coloured wig, 'welcome to Pop Kids . . .'

And so the show began. It was noisy, it was loud, and it was funny but I barely saw or heard any of it until Brody sat down, all pink and flushed from her song and gave me the thumbs-up.

'And now,' Mrs Fryston announced, glancing at her running order, 'Alex and Lloyd are going to perform an original number by the Hairy Pants . . .'

There was some laughter from the audience at the name and a dirty look from Huw as Lloyd and I stepped nervously forward. 'Actually,' I stammered, 'there's been a change of plan. Due to . . . technical difficulties we are going to sing something else instead. We don't need any backing,' I added quickly to Luke who had his drumsticks poised ready. I looked at Lloyd and took his hand and nodded. 'After three,' I whispered and we began.

The words to my favourite hymn 'There Is a Green Hill Far Away' must have sounded weird that afternoon amongst all the pop songs but everyone listened intently as Lloyd and I sang our way through it, just as we had done last week on Easter Sunday. I was aware of Lloyd's voice tailing off halfway through and I realized he didn't know the words off by heart like me but I just carried on. My voice filled the room and my heart soared as it always did when I was singing words that meant something to me. As I sang I thought of Daniel up in Heaven  and I hoped he was watching and I hoped he'd be proud of his little sister.

At the end, there was a silence and I thought for a second Lloyd had been right and we should just not have gone on but then everyone broke into applause and Caitlin stood up and shouted 'Encore!' More embarrassing still was other people joined her, even Mum and Dad. Even Huw.

Mrs Fryston walked on stage, still clapping, and when she congratulated us I'm sure there was a tear in her eye. 'Well, talk about talent!' she gushed.

'I suppose that wasn't so bad,' Lloyd admitted as we returned to our seats and Elvis took centre stage. 'You were pretty rubbish, though. I had to carry you . . .'

'Thanks.'

We took our places again and Lloyd whispered: 'I thought your mum was funny, wearing that T-shirt.'

'What T-shirt?' I whispered back.

'Didn't you see? It's the same one as yours—it says Bad Girl on it!'

'No!'

Half rising, I peered into the audience and he was right—Mum was wearing an identical top to mine! So that was why she wanted to know which one I'd be wearing. Mum saw me looking and grinned, pointing proudly to the slogan. I couldn't believe it. I smiled back, knowing it was her way of telling me she loved me.

'Watch this—this is going to be epic,' Lloyd said as Reggie, wearing a white sparkly Elvis suit stuffed with cushions waddled on to centre stage.

Reggie held his arms out over his head and started clapping. 'Now before I begin I want y' all to put your hands together like this, ladies and gen'lemen, boys and girls,' he said in a dreadful American drawl. 'I wanna hear it for the best darned After School club in the country . . .'

Everyone laughed and cheered. The back row where I was sitting stamped on the floor, making the chairs rattle. And guess who was stamping and cheering the loudest?

Epilogue

Life at After School club is totally different for me now. Either Dad or Caitlin pick me up at the end of the session like all the other kids and Mum stays on to tidy up and plan things like all the other members of staff. It keeps the boundaries clearer, Mrs Fryston says. Mrs Fryston has given me a special role, though. I help any new kids settle in because I know the ropes so well. She told me nobody else could do it better, which made Mum swell with pride. It is easy to see why Mrs Fryston is a leader—she is so good with people of all ages.

Helping the new kids means I don't spend so much time on the craft table with Mum any more but I am happy about that. It lets Brandon have some one-to-one time with her because I don't think he gets much from his mum and I know how *that* feels. Brandon is still a bit wary of me but he let me help him the other day when he fell in the cloakroom and Sammie has at least stopped calling me Mary, so I know I must be doing something right.

The activities have returned to normal at After School club since Pop Kids. Or as normal as they get with kids like Reggie and Brody around. Reggie started the **E-pals Challenge of the Day** a few weeks ago. The idea was everyone had to take it in turns to find a particular kind of e-pal to write to. His challenge was to find the weirdest e-pal, because Fatmuddyboy wouldn't stop writing to him so he said there must be more of them out there and it wasn't fair he should get lumbered. Lloyd's was to find one who had the longest or shortest name, Brody's for an e-pal the same birthday as one of us. When it was my turn to think of something, I suggested writing to people who lived in places beginning with 'W'.

'Huh! I thought you'd have gone for people who live on green hills far away,' Lloyd had teased. He says he'll never get over the trauma of singing hymns during Pop Kids but you wouldn't know it to look at him.

Brody had nudged him hard in the ribs. She knew what I was up to.

So that was how I began writing to Jolene in Washington, Tyne and Wear. It was just a couple of lines at first—how are you doing? that kind of thing—then the e-mails became longer and longer until we were back to how it was and I bet you Reggie's Elvis wig that if she walked through the door this second we'd be best friends again. I know from some of the things  Jolene writes that she still gets into trouble, but I'm not as scared of that now. There's more to Jolene than a bad temper. If she did get into a strop again, I would react better this time and try to calm her down before she got to boiling point. I'm a lot more tuned in to how people's brains work these days since my big talk with Caitlin.

Like Mum's, for example.

We are so much closer since I found out that Daniel was only an angel after he died and not before. Don't get me wrong, Mum and I still fall out over things like my clothes and untidiness but now if she says something like, 'Daniel would never do that,' I think to myself, Yes, he would, and that stops me being too rude back.

It's funny, when I think of Daniel, I think of him as he would be now, if he were alive, and not like the curly-haired kid in the mangled photograph on my dressing table. I imagine him as really tall with a spotty face, because that would be realistic for his age. He'd be in the Hairy Pants with Huw and they'd scowl at everything together. At home, he'd wear really manky clothes that Mum despaired of and he'd stick up for me and my tops. He'd be an ace older brother, though he'd have to go some way to beat Caitlin. Caitlin's just the best, though she keeps coming out with some divvy ideas.

She reckons during the summer holidays she's going to take me to Covent Garden and make me sing outside the Royal Opera House. According to her, we'd get so much money from rich American tourists she wouldn't have to find a summer job. I told her she has no chance because I'll be at After School club. The theme is 'Get Active' and when I mentioned to Jolene in my last e-mail activities included girls' football she said that was it, she was coming to ZAPS on the next bus. I wouldn't miss that for the world.

Do You Know an Alex?

Do you know someone who reminds you of Alex? Maybe one of your friends has a parent who's a teacher or an After School Club helper? Perhaps you have a long-distance e-pal? Or do you know somebody who's a great singer and has a story about a memorable performance?

If you have a story, send it to the After School Club website and we'll print the best stories and find out who is the biggest Alex of all!

www.oup.com/uk/children/afterschoolclub

starring Sammie ...

My life's a mess!

My dad's left home, all my mum cares about is going clubbing, and my sisters are a complete pain in the you-know-where.

As if that's not bad enough, I've just told a big fat lie, and I don't know how I'm going to get out of it. How would you get £100 by Monday?

At least things are normal at the After School Club, well, so far, anyway . . .

ISBN 0 19 275247 2

After School Club

starring Brody . . .

My family's so screwed-up!

You'd think my life was hectic enough, what with my modelling, school work, private tuition and After School Club—but now I've got my niece to stay. I'm trying to be nice to her but it turns out she has some major issues with me—I mean, big time.

I thought taking her to After School Club would help, but it just ain't happening . . .

ISBN 0 19 275248 0

After School Club

starring Jolene . . .

Ask me if I'm bothered!

I can't believe Mum's going on holiday without me. Well, if she thinks I'm going to stay at Nan's while she's away, she's got another think coming. I'm outta here.

Think I'll go and see me mate Alex and have a little holiday of my own – at least she'll be pleased to see me.

It's gonna be mint going to her After School Club again, just as long as they don't call the police and send me home . . .

ISBN 0 19 275250 2